"Surveillance cameras."

Sebastian flattened against the door, his eyes searching the control panel. Suddenly he hunched over, lunged for the panel and pushed a button. The red lights on the cameras went dark. A second later, he wrapped Leanne in his arms. "Are you all right?"

"I think so," Leanne said. "But we've got to hurry." The room on the other side of the observation window was now flooding with light. All along, while everyone tried to discourage her, she had persisted. And if she'd ever trusted her intuition, she did now. Because that same intuition was screaming at her... beyond that observation window, she and Sebastian would find all their answers. And, at last, they would really know the face of the enemy.

ABOUT THE AUTHOR

Lynn Leslie is actually the pseudonym for a very talented writing team, Sherrill Bodine and Elaine Sima, who live with their families outside Chicago, Illinois. Authors of Regencies and mainstream novels, both admit that romantic suspense is among their favorite genres.

Books by Lynn Leslie

HARLEQUIN INTRIGUE
129–STREET OF DREAMS

HARLEQUIN SUPERROMANCE
485–DEFY THE NIGHT

Don't miss any of our special offers. Write to us at the following address for information on our newest releases.

Harlequin Reader Service
P.O. Box 1397, Buffalo, NY 14240
Canadian address: P.O. Box 603,
Fort Erie, Ont. L2A 5X3

The Last Good-Night

Lynn Leslie

Harlequin Books

TORONTO • NEW YORK • LONDON
AMSTERDAM • PARIS • SYDNEY • HAMBURG
STOCKHOLM • ATHENS • TOKYO • MILAN
MADRID • WARSAW • BUDAPEST • AUCKLAND

To Jim and John: for all our tomorrows

Harlequin Intrigue edition published August 1992

ISBN 0-373-22192-4

THE LAST GOOD-NIGHT

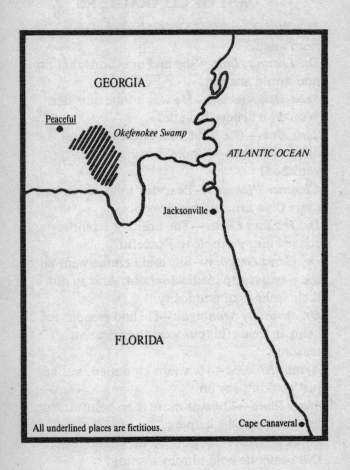

GEORGIA

Peaceful

Okefenokee Swamp

ATLANTIC OCEAN

Jacksonville

FLORIDA

All underlined places are fictitious.

Cape Canaveral

CAST OF CHARACTERS

Peaceful, Georgia—The town was clearly misnamed.

Dr. Leanne Hunt—She had questions that no one would answer.

Sebastian Kincaid—He was a lone outsider. Would he believe Leanne?

Jane Doe—The dead woman started it all.

Marcus Jacobs—Where did he go when he vanished?

Clarence Pickerell—Peaceful's mortician had more than arms up his sleeves.

Dr. William Lucas—The brilliant scientist coaxed many people to Peaceful.

Dr. Carla Gregory—She and Leanne went all the way back to medical school. And so did their feelings of animosity.

Dr. Anthony Montague—He had reasons for being in Peaceful, but were they the *real* reasons?

Arthur Kincaid—He was a kind man, but he just couldn't say no.

Mary Rand—She was more than helpful. But just *who* was she helping?

Louis Fontain—He popped up at odd times. Did someone hold him by a string?

Chapter One

Dr. Leanne Hunt didn't really want to observe the procedure taking place in pathology, but she felt it was her duty. It was a final service she could perform for Jane Doe.

After scrubbing quickly, Leanne donned a surgical gown, then drew latex gloves tightly over her fingers. She'd been on duty in the emergency room the night an elderly woman had been found unconscious in the bus station. For no good reason, and to the astonishment of her colleagues, she felt responsible for the woman who had no identification. There had been nothing to give the woman a name, a life, or a family. When Jane Doe's condition began to deteriorate Leanne haunted her room. At the end, only Leanne felt the need to stay by the stranger's bedside.

No one should die alone. Leanne had made a vow to herself in medical school that she would never allow that to happen while she was in charge.

This inquiry brought it all back. She'd been called away to another emergency, and by the time she returned her Jane Doe was gone. Carla had done a routine autopsy determining death by natural causes and

Leanne, although saddened, had thought no more about it until now.

Now there was a chance Jane Doe could be identified. If Carla could make this positive ID for the family in Tennessee who had gotten a court order to have the body exhumed, then among all the missing people in the United States, this woman would be one less. Leanne had her fingers crossed.

Taking a deep breath, she shouldered her way through the swinging doors to the autopsy room in the pathology department. This was her least favorite part of the hospital. Autopsies meant death and death meant failure. The first time Leanne worked on a cadaver in medical school she'd had to still a strong inner trembling in her stomach. Death was the enemy. You fought it, held it at bay, defeated it any way possible. William told her she was an excellent doctor because she understood this so well. But death had defeated her with Jane Doe.

She carefully averted her eyes from the stainless steel table and concentrated on Dr. Carla Gregory's hunched back. Carla looked up, startled by the swish of the closing door. "Leanne, what are you doing here? I'm nearly finished."

"I thought I should be here since I signed the death certificate."

"Yeah, I remember. I was working late that night. There ... finished." Carla grunted, throwing the scalpel into a stainless steel bowl; the clank of metal reverberated in the small silent room.

Finally, unavoidably, Leanne looked down at Jane Doe's body. The narrow, lined face, with the soft, kind mouth, lay in repose as still and white-gray as it had been the night she died. Exactly the same.

Shock jolted through Leanne. "Wait!" she demanded, gripping Carla's gloved wrist. "Carla, this woman died over three months ago but the body appears perfectly preserved."

Carla shrugged, her eyes tired above the surgical mask. "Yeah, it's a pretty good job. Embalming is an art these days. Seen enough?"

"No." She crossed to the supply cabinet. "This is weird. Do two more slides for me. One skin and one hair."

"Come on, Leanne, what's the deal? I've got more than enough for a positive ID. I want to get out of here." Carla patted perspiration from her brow with a white cloth. "I've got a load of work waiting in the lab."

"Just two more for me to study. I've never seen anything like this."

"No kidding? There aren't too many three-month-old cadavers hanging around here..." Carla laughed harshly.

Leanne turned away, Carla's sarcasm rankling. It reminded her of why they'd never been friendly even though they'd been in the same class in med school. Not that Leanne had had time for friends, or anything else, for that matter. She'd spent all her time studying or tutoring to make a little extra cash. Still, she and Carla just had nothing in common except medicine. Carla was abrasive and sarcastic. Nonetheless, Leanne had to admit she was a first-rate pathologist. Leanne had complete confidence in her evaluations and William thought her outstanding in her field.

That was something else they had in common—Dr. William Lucus. Unconsciously Leanne's hands unclenched and her body relaxed. *Dear William.* He was the reason she'd made it through school. And apparently he'd meant a lot to Carla too. For here they both were, at Peaceful Community Hospital in Peaceful, Georgia, on the edge of the Okefenokee Swamp, just because William Lucus had asked them to come.

"There! Just for you," Carla said. Her eyes were crinkled up at the corners and Leanne knew that behind the surgical mask her mouth was curled in a patronizing smile. "Happy now? Can we finally lay this poor woman to rest?"

"Of course," Leanne muttered, taking the slides from Carla's outstretched hand. "I'll leave you to finish. Thank you, Carla."

Carla answered with another grunt, drawing the sheet over Jane Doe's body for the last time.

Leanne stripped off her surgical garb and dumped it in the bin before checking her watch. She was already fifteen minutes late for rounds. Grabbing her white medical coat, she struggled into it. As she dashed out into the corridor, she collided with Lewis Fontain, who was pushing an empty gurney.

Lewis just prevented her from falling by quickly stepping aside; the gurney crashed against the wall. "Hey, slow down, Dr. Hunt," he warned. "You're goin' to hurt yourself."

"Sorry, Lewis. My fault." She laughed breathlessly, embarrassed to have been so careless.

He glanced down at her right hand; it clutched the slides tightly. "Goin' to the lab, huh? Just been there myself. Dr. Gregory ain't there."

"I know." Leanne shoved the slides into the pocket of her white coat. "I'm supposed to be on rounds right now. By the way, Lewis, will you please help the floor nurse move Mr. Jacobs from room thirty-six to forty-five?"

"Done already." He smiled, his bushy, sandy-colored mustache spreading across his face. He rocked back on his heels, holding the righted gurney in front of him. "The duty nurse last night told me you wanted it done. Did it first thing when I got back from breakfast."

"Thank you, Lewis. Doing double duty again? What would we do without you?" She liked Lewis best of all the orderlies; he was the most cooperative and certainly the most unfailingly cheerful. Another glance at her watch sent her striding quickly yet more carefully down the corridor. "See you later," floated on the air behind her.

She was late but took the time to stop at her office and place the slides in the top drawer of her desk. After rounds, she'd go to the lab and take a look at these herself, she thought. Leanne had seen death more times than she liked to think about, but she'd never seen . . . of course, Carla was right. She didn't usually see a body again three months later. Maybe she was making a mountain out of a molehill.

True to Lewis's word, Leanne found Marcus Jacobs settled in the private room. He was asleep, so she didn't disturb him. Glancing through his chart, she was disappointed that his test results weren't in yet.

But his prognosis didn't look good. If it all went the way she feared, he would be more comfortable in this room during his treatments.

Her other patients were more routine which made her a lot happier: a young boy with asthma who would go home tomorrow, Peaceful's only dental hygienist who was recovering from gallbladder surgery, the fullback from the local high school football team, who'd suffered a dislocated shoulder in Friday's win, so it didn't hurt *too* much, and Arthur Kincaid who was going through physical therapy after hip replacement surgery. She'd known Arthur Kincaid slightly even before he'd come to the hospital. He was one of the residents of Shady Rest Retirement Village, William's model senior citizen community.

Leanne always saved Arthur for last; that way she could spend more time with him. He was such a sweet, old gentleman, flirting outrageously with her every chance he got. Responding to his fulsome flattery stirred vague regrets that her single-minded pursuit of her degree and career had given her no time for emotional ties to anyone, except William. She'd nearly forgotten there was anything else in life worth pursuing besides work.

Looking forward to her usual repartee with the eighty-two-year-old Arthur, Leanne smiled broadly and pushed his door open. She stopped as if she had walked into a glass wall.

A man, a stranger who was sitting beside the bed, rose slowly to his feet. "Can I help you?"

Arthur glanced around, somewhat bewilderedly, then his thin face widened in a mischievous grin. Arthur had had no visitors except William his entire stay.

He'd insisted he had no relatives to be called, but Leanne now realized that couldn't be true. The stranger was looking at her with Arthur Kincaid's wide, soft brown eyes.

"At last, my favorite physician, the beautiful Dr. Hunt," Arthur chuckled, stretching out one thin arm. "Come meet my nephew, Sebastian Kincaid. He came from Cape Canaveral to see me. He's an astrophysicist with NASA. I sat in the audience when he got his doctorate from MIT. He's following in his old uncle's footsteps," Arthur said, pride written all over his face. He peered up at his nephew.

Sebastian smiled, moving quickly around the bed to shake Leanne's hand. "How do you do, Dr. Hunt?"

"Mr. Kincaid." She nodded, slowly pulling her hand away and thrusting it into her jacket pocket. Sebastian Kincaid was of medium height and slender build, but there was an energy in his movement, a forcefulness in his wide coffee gaze, and a cleft in his square chin that deepened with his smile. A strength in his voice made him appear larger than he really was and sparked the air around him. That spark stirred to life something inside Leanne and suddenly her throat was hot and tight.

"He's a chip off the old block, isn't he, Dr. Hunt?" Arthur's voice broke through her thoughts. "Ever told you about my nephew here?"

"No, Arthur." Grateful for an excuse to move, Leanne passed Sebastian and went to the bed. "I didn't know you had any family close by."

Arthur reached out one hand, lightly freckled with age spots, and she took it, holding it firmly. "Can't think why I didn't tell you about Sebastian. He's my brother Joseph's boy. A scientist like all the Kincaids . . . used to be a famous scientist myself.''

"I know. You discovered a supernova." She smiled. She did so enjoy Arthur's determined zest in the face of all he was going through! She slid a chair next to the bed. Sebastian moved to his uncle's other side but remained standing. Their eyes met briefly.

She noticed that Sebastian's light brown hair was shaggy at the back as if he needed a haircut. "I was very impressed when you told me about the supernova," Leanne teased, looking at Arthur.

"Knew I'd done some bragging." He laughed. "Sebastian here has heard it all, but he's staying a few days so I can bore him some more with my old space stories."

"Uncle Arthur, it's been a long time. We have a lot of catching up to do. Maybe Dr. Hunt can tell us when you'll be released?" Those soft brown eyes questioned her.

"Your uncle needs at least three more days with the physical therapist." She answered clearly, but that tight hot feeling still hovered at the back of her throat.

"The only good thing about this place is you, Dr. Hunt," Arthur groaned. "Well, Sebastian, you're going to have to run out to Shady Rest and bring me some things. Old books and files I want to show you."

"Fine." Sebastian placed a hand on his uncle's slim shoulder. "How do I get there?"

The creases in Arthur's brow deepened. "I'm no good on directions anymore. Dr. Hunt, can you help us out here?"

This was the day Leanne had planned to drive out to Shady Rest. She had something very special to give to William. And now, she had another reason to go. She wanted to discuss Jane Doe with him. She discussed everything with William. He was her mentor, true friend, and the only real family she had.

Sometimes she stayed for hours talking with William. Did she really want to put a time limit on her visit? Yet, Arthur was looking at her with such sweet earnestness she couldn't disappoint him, even though the idea of spending more time with his nephew was oddly disquieting.

"I'm going out there myself. I'll take Sebastian."

Arthur broke into a wide grin and raised her hand, pressing his lips against it. "You're a little darling! Isn't she, Sebastian?"

Flushing, Leanne stood and deliberately avoided Sebastian's eyes. She felt foolish at being called *little*. She was five-eight in her stocking feet and had been since she was a teenager. She'd always considered herself an amazon.

"I'll check out, then meet Sebastian in front." She forced herself to look at Sebastian and smiled faintly. "It's a green Buick. Give me fifteen minutes."

He nodded, his wide, brown eyes studying her closely. The odd disquiet she felt deepened to mild regret. Why had she offered him a ride? She wasn't looking forward to forty minutes in the car with those knowing eyes.

"WHAT A FINE-LOOKING woman, eh, Sebastian?" Arthur sighed, settling back on his pillows after Leanne left the room. "If I were fifty years younger, I'd grab that one up." Shaking his head, Arthur laughed, the robust full laugh Sebastian remembered so well. "It's not too late for you. I'd be proud to have her for a niece."

Before Sebastian could respond, Arthur's eyes, so much like his own—they were the Kincaid legacy—narrowed and he elbowed his way to sit up straighter in bed. "What am I saying! You're already taken. Where's Jessica? Why didn't she come and visit me, too?"

Sebastian stood at the foot of the bed, gripping the railing so tightly that the cool metal bit into his palms. It had been a very long time since he'd talked about Jessica.

"Uncle Arthur, Jessica died in an accident at her lab four years ago," he said quietly.

To his infinite relief Arthur didn't ask any other questions. He just sat for a minute, shaking his head.

"Sorry to hear it, Sebastian. I always liked your wife." He shrugged. "But life goes on." He swung his legs down to the floor. "Help me over to that chair by the window, will you?" Settling in, he sighed. "Ah...that's better. Now, where was I? Oh, yes." The mottled hands plucked at the gray chenille robe that covered his legs. "Are you dating anyone?"

"I haven't had the time. I've been concentrating on my research for NASA." Sighing, Sebastian relaxed enough to answer. This was not a subject he ever dealt with successfully. If he'd dealt more successfully with his relationship with Jessica, maybe, just maybe, Jessica would still be alive.

"You need to find the time. You're not getting any younger...happened to me. Work was everything. When you realize it isn't, it's too late. I'm telling you, you should grab Dr. Hunt while you can."

The outrageous suggestion made him laugh out loud, and to his surprise he realized that laughter made it easier to think about Jessica and his life without her. But his guilt still lingered. He should have been there for her. That he'd been across the country at a shuttle launch when she'd died would haunt him forever.

Forcing that thought away, he smiled down at his uncle. "What I'm going to do is grab a ride with your Dr. Hunt." He clasped Arthur's shoulder, saddened to feel how little flesh covered the bones. "I'll be back soon."

Sebastian pushed the elevator button and checked his watch. Dr. Hunt should be ready by now. Smiling to himself, he shook his head; a woman waiting beside him gave him a startled glance and moved away.

He stepped into the elevator alone and as the doors slid shut, laughed out loud. Maybe Uncle Arthur was right. He needed to get on with his life. He needed to think about something besides NASA, about... someone. And, Uncle Arthur was also correct about Leanne Hunt. She was attractive, even though her light blond hair was pulled back too severely from the fragile bones of her face. Still, it was a very pretty face with nice, clear blue eyes. He liked the way they'd become clearer and brighter when she'd smiled at Arthur. Her bedside manner was charming; most doctors could take lessons from her.

She was definitely a woman with possibilities—for someone. But, not him. If Sebastian ever got on with his life it wouldn't involve a Leanne Hunt. She was clearly another single-minded professional as Jessica had been. He needed someone very different from

Jessica. He wasn't going to open himself to that gut-wrenching pain again.

HER CLEAR BLUE EYES were hidden behind large dark glasses when Sebastian climbed into the car. He felt a tug of regret that he couldn't see them. She gave him a faint smile as he buckled his seat belt, then she concentrated on driving. He watched her hands on the steering wheel. Her fingers were long and thin, the bones of her wrists small. For a tall woman she was amazingly delicate. He suddenly remembered how her fair skin had flushed light pink when Arthur had called her a little darling.

"Is something wrong, Mr. Kincaid?" she asked quietly, giving him a side-glance.

Realizing he had been staring at her, he looked away, studying the Georgia countryside. They'd left the town behind and were traveling over sandy flatland, with fields of peanuts and sweet potatoes. "No, on the contrary, everything's great. I've found Uncle Arthur again. We lost touch five years ago. When he called, it was like we'd just seen one another yesterday."

Glancing at her, he noticed that her fingertips were white from gripping the wheel.

"Are you close to your uncle?"

Sebastian smiled, remembering. "He bought me my first telescope and my first books on astronomy. I was hooked. My parents weren't pleased. They're geneticists and wanted me to continue the tradition. But Uncle Arthur insisted that space was the final frontier."

Sebastian was strangely pleased to see that he had made her smile. "What about you? How long have you been Arthur's doctor?"

"Since I came here a year ago. William Lucus, who owns Shady Rest Retirement Village, is a good friend of mine and recommended me to Arthur."

"He likes you. You have a nice bedside manner," he said simply. He was surprised to see her delicate cheeks blush again. Humidity was causing wisps of hair to curl freely against her skin. "Hip replacement is no picnic at his age." He continued in a different vein, wanting to put her at ease. "What's the prognosis?"

"His physical therapy is going well. I'm not unduly concerned." She glanced at him, as if afraid to look him full in the face before she continued. "I'm sure he'll do even better now that you're here. How long will you be staying?"

There was something in her tone that caused a knot of suspicion to form in his gut. "I'm not sure." He studied her pretty profile—the short, slightly turned up nose and full upper lip. "I can't stay away from my research too long."

"Of course not. I understand perfectly... here we are." She halted the car in front of a white miniature antebellum mansion, in a parklike setting of magnolias and moss-draped trees. Red-roofed white villas were visible behind it.

Leanne hastily opened her door and stepped out. As Sebastian followed, two ideas struck him: Leanne Hunt was being evasive about Arthur's condition, and for some reason he made her nervous.

When they entered the lobby of Shady Rest's administration building the blast of cool air was a relief.

Self-consciously tightening the coil of hair at her nape, Leanne looked at Sebastian. "Follow me. I'll find someone to help you."

She didn't wait for him to answer, but walked quickly toward William's office. She decided she needed to add Freon to her car; she had certainly felt warm on the drive. It must be the air-conditioning, she thought. She refused to think the heat had anything to do with the man traveling with her.

No, it couldn't have anything to do with the haunted sadness deep in his dark eyes or the odd appeal of the whimsical smile on his chiseled mouth. Taking a long, deep breath of fresh air and lengthening her stride, she put some distance between herself and the object of her most surprising curiosity.

"Hi, Mary. Is William in?" she called. She approached the desk outside the dark oak double doors to William's office.

Mary Rand looked up, her silver-gray hair haloing her small face. "Leanne, dear, what a pleasant surprise." She stood, nearly quivering with efficiency. "William is in conference, but I'll tell him you're here."

"No, don't bother him. Mary, I'd like you to meet Sebastian Kincaid, Arthur's nephew. He's come to pick up some things for his uncle."

Sebastian stepped forward, smiling. "Nice to meet you, Mary. I hope you can help me."

Leanne could see that Mary responded much the same as she had to the magnetic, intangible quality Sebastian possessed.

"Why, I'd be delighted," she gushed, bustling around the desk. "Arthur and I are good friends. In fact, his villa is just a few doors from mine. I'll take you over there right now. Leanne, dear, if William comes out of his conference, tell him I'll be right back."

Placing a small hand on Sebastian's arm, Mary led him toward the outer doors. Leanne noticed he didn't glance back but was totally engrossed in whatever Mary was saying to him.

Maybe that's why Sebastian Kincaid got to her. When he looked at people it was as if they were the absolute center of his attention. Maybe astronomers developed that intensity after peering through telescopes for years. Still, being so closely studied was disquieting for her after years of isolation. The only person who'd ever gotten close enough to penetrate her reserve was William. She'd have to stop being so sensitive, she thought. Maybe it was time to let some other people into her life.

"I wasn't expecting you!"

She turned at the sound of William's voice. He was opening his door to allow another man to exit. The stranger was dwarfed by William's impressive height and physique. William was in excellent shape, particularly for a man of his age.

"At last, the two of you can meet," William boomed, motioning Leanne closer. "Dr. Leanne Hunt, Dr. Anthony Montague of the Meridan Foundation."

"Dr. Hunt, William has spoken of you often. I am glad to meet you." Anthony Montague gave her a firm, but brief, handshake. "William, I must be off." He nodded to Leanne then left, moving through the outer doors and down the hall to the front entrance.

Leanne had made a point of learning how to remember faces; it helped when dealing with patients' families. She had seen Anthony Montague before, but she couldn't remember where. And there was nothing outstanding about him to jog her memory. He was of medium height and slender build, with dark hair and eyes. That could describe anyone, even Sebastian Kincaid, but she doubted anyone had ever forgotten a meeting with Sebastian.

"I've seen Dr. Montague somewhere before," Leanne muttered, looking up at William. "Can you think where?"

He shrugged his broad shoulders before embracing her in a warm, tight hug. "It's so good to see you. To what do I owe this visit?"

He led her to a stuffed chair and then leaned on the edge of his desk and crossed his long legs.

When Leanne had first seen Dr. William Lucus standing, without notes, to give his introductory lecture on geriatrics, she had thought he looked like a god. His mane of pure white hair had framed the strong bones of his face. The impressive breadth of his shoulders and his proud carriage made him appear younger than his age. Ten years later he still didn't look any older. In the intervening years, Leanne had not only seen beneath the impressive facade to the wonderfully giving man, but she had also come to love him.

"I have something for you, William." She opened her handbag and removed an envelope, holding it out to him. "It's the last payment on the loan you gave me to finish medical school."

He took the envelope from her hand and turned it over before placing it on his desk. "You've already repaid me by becoming one of the finest physicians I know," he said softly in the rich, deep voice she knew so well. He had helped her through the rough waters of med school. He was there for her, not only as her academic advisor, but also as her friend, when no one else had been available, not even her parents. They had been too involved in their own new lives after their divorce, but William had been there.

"I don't think I can ever repay my debts to you." Leanne stood to face him. "You're the only person I've ever been able to rely on besides myself."

"And I'll always be here for you." He squeezed her hand. "Now tell me what else is bothering you. I know that stubborn tilt to your chin. I noticed it the first time you disagreed with a lab experiment. So tell me."

She laughed. His familiar teasing dissolved away the last of the tension she'd been feeling all day. Now that she had someone to share her fears with, they seemed almost silly. "Remember the Jane Doe I told you about? Well, the court order came through and Carla did the tests. I observed."

He raised his bushy eyebrows.

"Yes, I know." She shook her head. "But I felt I should and, William, it was amazing! The body was in a state of perfect preservation."

He shrugged, much as Carla had. "Embalming is quite advanced these days. If Pickerell and Pickerell did the job, I'm sure it was excellent. Clarence is a third generation mortician. I knew both his grandfather and his father."

"Then you don't think this is anything outside the ordinary?" she asked, a little thread of doubt refusing to give way.

"I wouldn't think so. How is Arthur's physical therapy going?"

The abrupt change of subject startled her. "Arthur? He's doing well. He should be home in a few days."

"And his Alzheimer's disease?"

At the question, Leanne paced across the oriental rug that lay over the darkly stained pine floor. "I'm afraid it's progressing. In fact, his distant memory is getting stronger while his present memory increasingly fails. He called his nephew to visit him."

"Nephew! I didn't know he had any family." William walked around the desk and lowered himself into his chair.

"Sebastian hadn't heard from his uncle in over five years. But when he called, Sebastian said it was as if they'd just seen one another."

Frowning, William leaned back. "Damn it to hell!" he boomed, slamming his fist against the arm of the chair. "I've been fighting death my entire life. Here at Shady Rest I see so many men and women with fine minds who still have so much to offer society but who are betrayed by their bodies. And I can't do anything but rage against the waste."

The usual healthy pink of his face reddened alarmingly and Leanne touched his arm. "We all feel that way, William."

Nodding, he placed his hand over hers. "Have you told his nephew?"

"Not yet. But I think I should. There may be other relatives to be consulted when Arthur deteriorates."

"Yes . . . Leanne, there is some—"

The office door flew open, interrupting him. Mary Rand's face glowed with a wide smile. Sebastian followed her in. His eyes paused briefly on Leanne and William's clasped hands.

For some reason, the gesture that had never seemed so intimate before suddenly made her self-conscious. She slowly slid her hand free of William's and let it drop to her side.

Leanne stood back while Mary introduced Sebastian and William with her quick, breathless efficiency. William genially offered Sebastian the hospitality of Shady Rest's guest cottage during his visit. For the first time in Leanne's experience, another man wasn't overshadowed by William's impressive bearing. Most of the men she knew, even those years younger, faded in comparison.

William's next appointment, an elderly couple who wished to look at a villa, arrived, so Mary shepherded Leanne and Sebastian out. But not before William gave Leanne a parting kiss on the cheek as he always did. Why did this, too, suddenly seem so intimate, so personal?

She hadn't thought of intimacy, of sex, in . . . she didn't know how long. Who had the time for intimacy? Who had time to devote to developing a relationship? Certainly she didn't. And why would that fact fill her with such regret today?

Her heart pounding in her chest, she practically ran toward her car. She slid in, started the engine, and turned the air-conditioning up to maximum, before

Sebastian could slam his door shut. She'd been right earlier, she thought. It wasn't pleasant being scrutinized by those knowing eyes.

"Shady Rest is quite impressive. Have you known William Lucus long?" Sebastian finally broke the silence that was growing marked since they left the retirement village.

"He was my advisor in medical school." Her tone was sharper than usual. She didn't want to discuss William with this man. He made her feel unsure of herself in ways she hadn't felt for years.

He nodded once then stared out the window for the rest of the ride. What was the matter with the man? Didn't he know how to make polite conversation? Didn't she?

She was usually better at making small talk than this. No doubt Sebastian was changing his mind about her bedside manner. She had found his remark about that embarrassing and had even felt herself blush like a silly schoolgirl. She must be working too hard, she thought now. She was tired or she wouldn't feel so edgy. Maybe she was edgy because she had to give Sebastian bad news about his uncle. But now was not the time. She'd set up an appointment in her office where she was always in control of the situation.

She caught herself stealing a glance at his profile. Sebastian had a firm, square chin and a perfect patrician nose. But when she caught herself looking down to see if he wore a wedding ring she got herself firmly in hand. She was stunned to discover that the effect he had on her was making her forget the last nagging worry about Jane Doe.

Leanne tightened her jaw. William would, no doubt, recognize the gesture. He was right. When she thought something was wrong, she couldn't let go of it. She had never let anything get in the way of work before and she wouldn't be completely satisfied now until she came up with an explanation for herself about Jane Doe's body. She'd simply ignore the odd little twists her thoughts were inexplicably taking today and concentrate on the problem at hand.

When they reached the hospital, Sebastian turned to her. "Thank you for the ride, Dr. Hunt. It was very interesting." With that odd parting remark, he smiled and got out of the car.

She watched him walk away. Her first impression had been correct; he definitely made her nervous. Relieved to be alone, she headed toward the hospital doors herself. She signed in and checked her messages. That done, she could finally head to her office. There was some time now before late rounds. She'd just take a look at those slides so she could put Jane Doe out of her mind.

Her windows faced north and didn't get the afternoon sun, so her office was dim when she went in. She flipped on the overhead lights before going to the desk to pull open the top desk drawer.

She blinked. She pushed aside a tablet of manila paper and two white hospital envelopes. She flipped on the desk lamp and tilted the metal shade so the light shone directly into the drawer, illuminating even the darkest corners. But it was no use. Jane Doe's slides were gone.

Chapter Two

Leanne sat back hard in her swivel chair and stared blankly at the desk drawer. The slides she'd so carefully placed in this drawer only six hours before were gone. Just to be certain, she opened every other drawer and looked inside. Then she went back to the top drawer and took each thing out one at a time.

The slides were definitely gone, not just hiding under papers or envelopes. They had vanished into thin air! How did they get out of her desk? Had someone taken them? Who? And why? The only answer brought her to her feet and sent her scurrying out into the corridor.

Carla looked up from her microscope when Leanne entered the lab. "What do you need, Leanne?"

"Did you take those Jane Doe slides out of my desk drawer?"

Carla raised her dark eyebrows in haughty defence. "First of all, I'm not in the habit of going through your desk." Easing back on her high stool, she crossed her legs. "Secondly, I have more slides than I can possibly need. What happened? Did you lose them?"

Folding her arms across her chest, Leanne stared at Carla's mocking face. She must be overly tired, she thought. Usually Carla's sarcasm rolled right over her. "Yes, I seem to have misplaced them. Could I take a look at the ones you have?"

"Sorry, I sent all my slides to Tennessee by messenger. The court was rather insistent that I move swiftly—unlike justice. I even faxed the dental X rays and fingerprints, what there were of them. That was probably enough for a positive ID anyway, without the slides." With a small grin, Carla leaned over her microscope again. "Oh, I forgot." She tilted her head and gave Leanne a sideways glance. "When Clarence Pickerell came to pick up the body, I told him how much you admired his work."

"Is Jane Doe still there?" Leanne asked quickly.

"I don't know." Carla shrugged. "Give Clarence a call."

Leanne would do better than that. She would see him herself. The tiny thread of doubt that had refused to give way even in the face of William's assurances began to twist and grow stronger. There was no reason those slides should be missing from her drawer. Not unless they might reveal something that someone didn't want Dr. Leanne Hunt to see. But that was crazy. No one but she had been even remotely interested in Jane Doe.

At the door, Leanne turned back one last time. "Carla, was there anything out of the ordinary about the Jane Doe slides?"

Carla didn't even bother to look up from the microscope. "Not particularly."

That gave Leanne pause. Carla had a great eye for spotting trouble. Nevertheless, Leanne needed to see for herself.

She drove hurriedly out to the stately and serene red brick Federal-style facade of Pickerell and Pickerell. The funeral home marked the very edge of town. Separate, set off to one side, was a small white chapel that often doubled as a marriage site for young eloping couples. It was postcard pretty with its lighted steeple and magnolia-lined walkway.

Smothering silence descended as Leanne shut the door to the mortuary. No one was in the reception area, so she followed the thickly carpeted hall past two parlors that were dark and vacant. There were no customers today.

The hall came to a T. Leanne turned right instinctively. The first office she peered into was empty, but the lights were on. That meant someone was around somewhere. She went to the end of the hallway, but when she tried another door, she found that office locked.

The sun had set and the light filtering in from the high window suddenly faded, leaving her in shadows. In the dimness Leanne turned to retrace her steps.

"May I help you?"

Her heartbeat exploded in her ears, and she gasped in shocked surprise, one hand flying to her throat.

Out of the molten darkness, Clarence Pickerell materialized. His black suit melted into the shadows so well that his long, pale face seemed disembodied. Fascinated, Leanne stared at his prominent hook nose and the dark hollows beneath his high cheekbones. The apparition spoke again.

"I am sorry I frightened you, Dr. Hunt," the mortician apologized, blinking his heavy-lidded eyes. "Is there something I can do for you?"

Drawing in a ragged breath, Leanne sighed. "I didn't hear you coming."

He glanced down. "Thick carpets you know. They make for a very restful silence."

"Of course." Leanne looked toward the light spilling out of the office behind him, suddenly eager to reach it. "Could we go to your office? I'd like to talk to you."

Bowing his head, he stepped aside so she might pass, which she did quickly. Her breathing was still a little unsteady as she slid into a chair.

Clarence Pickerell reminded her of every stereotype about morticians. Perhaps it was because the solemn voice, the placid expression and the slow movements were all ingrained so deeply they weren't just part of his professional conduct, but summed up his total personality.

He offered her a glass of water, which she accepted gratefully. Then he sat ramrod straight behind the desk and folded his hands on the blotter in front of him. "How may I help you?" he inquired.

"I'd like to see our Jane Doe."

The heavy-lidded eyes blinked again as he shook his head. "I am sorry but Jane Doe is no longer with us. I received word from the authorities not two hours ago that positive identification had been made. Delores Madison is, happily, now on her way to her final resting place, with her family where she belongs."

Disappointment was softened by relief. Jane Doe had a name, Delores Madison. Leanne was glad, but that twisted strand of doubt still nagged at her. "Mr. Pickerell, did you do anything different with Jane...I mean Delores Madison, when you processed her body? Anything that might have preserved it better?"

Slowly running one palm over his balding head, he blinked several times. "I don't recall laying Mrs. Madison to rest any differently than anyone else. Dr. Hunt, Pickerell has provided the finest in interment for over fifty years. Although Mrs. Madison had no family to be satisfied, I assure you we gave her the same excellent care we give all our clients."

"I'm sure you did." Leanne stood, holding out her hand. "Thank you for your time, Mr. Pickerell." She was surprised that his hand wasn't cold; on the contrary, it was warm and slightly moist.

Returning down the darkened corridor, the funeral home seemed comforting. She felt none of the eerie sensations she'd experienced earlier. Leanne realized how foolishly she was behaving, running all over town, asking questions about a body that had been buried for over three months. She must be overworked and overtired. Why else would she feel so off balance, as if something in the fabric of Peaceful, Georgia had suddenly altered, making a new pattern she couldn't follow?

The parking lot was dark. There was no funeral now, so there were no lights. And the lot seemed even darker because the moon hadn't risen above the tall moss-draped trees.

Leanne's heels clicked rhythmically on the concrete. Suddenly she stopped, listening. Yes, there it was behind her, a heavier footfall.

Bracing herself, she turned. But no one was there. There was nothing to see in the darkness except the light filtering through the drapes in Clarence Pickerell's office window. Silhouetted behind the drapes were two figures. Someone else must have been in the funeral parlor, after all.

Still uneasy, Leanne sprinted the last few yards to her car. She fumbled for a second with the lock before climbing in to safety. She relocked the door quickly and securely. She just needed to get a good night's sleep. Tomorrow she would solve the puzzle of the missing slides. There was, no doubt, some reasonable explanation. Still, right now, she couldn't imagine what it would be.

She kept glancing up at her rearview mirror as she pulled out of the parking lot. What did she expect to see? Leanne had always vaguely regretted that she wasn't more imaginative, but she liked cold hard facts. She was a scientist and naturally pragmatic on top of that. Since that was the case, why were her thoughts twisting and turning into such improbable avenues today? First, because of Jane Doe. Then Sebastian Kincaid.

Her hands tightened on the wheel when she realized that even in the face of the mysteriously missing slides, she hadn't quite shaken off the disturbing effect Sebastian Kincaid had on her.

"HAPPY BIRTHDAY, Uncle Arthur!" Sebastian declared, laying a present wrapped in blue and white paper on the bed. He was rewarded with a broad smile. Arthur's tired, brown eyes lightened and his hand touched the bright blue ribbon. "You shouldn't have done this, Sebastian. I forgot myself . . . can't be-lieve you remembered.''

"I'll never forget the first time you took me to Mount Palomar. It was your birthday and after din-ner you let me look through the big telescope. Re-member?''

"Of course I remember." Arthur laughed. "Seems like only yesterday. Knew right then you were going to be an astrophysicist." Pulling the gift onto his lap, Arthur tugged at the ribbon. "Now let's see what's in this box.''

Sebastian leaned against the window enjoying his uncle's pleasure at his simple gesture of gift giving. The package contained a book with the most recent pictures from the Hubble Space Telescope. "I've brought some footage of the last launch to show you. I'll find a VCR we can hook up to your TV.''

"I'll bet Dr. Hunt would enjoy seeing the film, too. You missed her today. She already made rounds.''

Sebastian smiled at his uncle's eager face. "Dr. Hunt strikes me as someone who doesn't relax much. I doubt she'll have the time.''

"Ask her will you, Sebastian? It's my birthday and all. Make it seem more like a party.''

The wistful tone won him over. If Uncle Arthur wanted Dr. Hunt, Sebastian would do his best. He doubted she'd take the time even if she had it. His in-stincts were usually on target.

The pretty doctor wasn't being entirely honest with him, he decided. First, she hadn't told him everything about Arthur's condition. That he fully intended to explore. The rest, including her nervousness with him, wasn't something he understood or wanted to deal with, no more than he wanted to deal with why, last night, he had dreamed about Jessica.

The same dream had haunted him every night for two months after her death. In the dream, he stumbled down darkened streets toward the bright glow ahead. Headlong in flight, he was always knocked down by the force of the explosion, its heat scorching his skin. He would struggle up to launch himself against the wall of firemen who prevented him from storming Jessica's lab. She was in there, in that inferno. He could see her face pressed to the window, her bright blond hair haloed by the scarlet flame.

But last night, the face pressed to the window had been Leanne Hunt's. Even now, he couldn't shake the feelings that dream had reawakened. Realistically, he knew Jessica's death hadn't happened that way. Maybe if he'd really been there his subconscious wouldn't have created such a horror-filled nightmare. Why had it added Leanne to the grisly scene now? Was there something too familiar about her that unleashed this flood of memories? If so, the less he saw of her, the better it would be for his peace of mind.

Nevertheless, a half an hour later, urged on by Arthur's eager insistence, he found himself looking for her. He was only doing this to please his uncle on his birthday, Sebastian told himself.

He finally found her at the first floor nurses' station. Like yesterday, small wisps of pale hair had broken from their bondage to curl around her cheeks. But unlike yesterday, there were dark purple smudges beneath her eyes. What or who had kept Dr. Hunt awake last night?

She glanced up and gave him a brief, almost wary, smile. "Hello, Sebastian."

"I've been looking for you with a message from Uncle Arthur." He leaned against the counter next to her. "It's his birthday and I've arranged to bring in some space footage to show him. He wants you to come and make it a party."

He saw the answer flicker through her clear blue eyes and resigned himself to disappointing his uncle. Straightening, he waited for her rejection.

"Yes, I'll come."

He didn't know who was more surprised, him or her.

Stepping back one pace, she hugged a clipboard to her chest as if already regretting her response. But it was too late to change her mind and she knew it.

"Can you wait about an hour? I have a conference with a patient before I can officially sign out for the evening."

"Sure. It will take me a while to set things up. We'll wait for you. The bakery isn't delivering the cake until dinner, anyway."

"You ordered a cake?" A smile, with the faintest resemblance to the blaze of glory she'd given Arthur yesterday, glimmered briefly on her face.

"Sure. What's a birthday party without cake? We'll see you later." He turned away, happy Arthur was getting his party and surprised at how much he was looking forward to it himself.

Sebastian Kincaid not only made her uneasy, he surprised her, she thought. A birthday cake! Somehow, a man who was that thoughtful about an elderly uncle's birthday didn't fit her idea of a high-powered careerist.

The biggest surprise of all was that she'd agreed to go. Was she doing it for Arthur or because her curiosity about his nephew needed to be satisfied? Sebastian's aura of tightly reined energy was strangely appealing. This spark of interest in the void of her personal life was as unexpected and disturbing as everything else that had happened in the last twenty-four hours. Maybe a few minutes of relaxation wouldn't hurt, particularly after she saw this final patient.

She looked at the report in her hands. In med school they didn't teach an easy way to break this kind of news. She paused outside Marcus Jacobs's room to take a deep breath and put on a reassuring face. She pushed the door open.

She recognized Dr. Anthony Montague even before he turned to face her. His handshake was as brief as before. "Dr. Hunt, good to see you." His hasty departure was equally quick. "Marcus, Joyce. I'll see you both soon." He gave a characteristic nod and was gone.

Leanne finally remembered why he seemed familiar. She *had* caught glimpses of him around the hospital before. But she'd never gotten a real look at him because he always seemed to be hurrying away.

"I just met Dr. Montague yesterday. Do you know him well?" she asked.

Joyce nodded, moving closer to the bed to take her husband's hand. "He's a friend." As if she couldn't bear another moment of waiting she continued bluntly, "Have you got the results?"

Leanne wasn't immune to their pain. She saw fear in Marcus's and Joyce's faces and knew she could do nothing to ease it. Instead, her words would deepen it, making it a part of them, of their lives, their future.

"The CAT scan showed a spot on the right lobe of the brain. However, the oncologist will want to be certain. I know this all seems overwhelming to you right now, but there is a plus. Dr. Fredricks is the best . . . and I know he'll do everything in his power to help you." She wanted to close her eyes against the agony in their faces.

Joyce carried their clasped hands to her trembling lips to press a kiss on her husband's knuckles.

"What is the treatment?" Marcus asked hoarsely, suddenly looking years older.

Marcus was forty years old and had three small sons at home. Leanne pushed that thought away. "Dr. Fredricks will be in to see you in a few minutes. He will explain the next stage of treatment."

"More chemotherapy and radiation," Marcus said bleakly, shaking his head. "Dr. Hunt, would you mind leaving us alone for a few minutes?"

Nodding, she turned away. At the door, she glanced back. They were holding one another, tears running down their cheeks.

She was glad she wouldn't have to tell them that exploratory surgery for this type of tumor was a pretty risky business. Fredricks had a lot of experience; he'd know the right words. She paged him and gave him the results, then asked him to wait before conferring with the Jacobses. They needed some time alone together.

Suddenly, Sebastian's invitation assumed greater importance. In a small community like Peaceful, every patient became a friend. She was so involved, it was always difficult to retain her objectivity. For the first time, she realized the value of professional detachment; it was to preserve her own sanity. Still, she'd never been able to maintain it past the first few visits with a patient, particularly not with Arthur.

There wasn't much else she could do for Arthur but share what little pleasures he had left. Seeing him deteriorate would be one of the hardest things she'd ever have to face. Powerless—that's how she felt sometimes. With all her expertise, with all science had to offer, there were still moments like this. No doubt she'd eventually get hardened and accept her limitations, but not just yet.

She needed to do something positive. After signing out, she stopped at the gift shop and bought a pink azalea for Arthur. Sometime very soon she had to talk to Sebastian about his uncle's condition. This wasn't the time. She saw that instantly when she entered Arthur's room. Both men were talking, totally engrossed as they flipped through a book.

She placed the flowerpot on the bedside table. "Happy birthday."

Before she could step back, Arthur took her hand, squeezing it. "You shouldn't have. It's enough to have the prettiest doctor in the hospital share my birthday. I haven't had a birthday party since I was twelve. Seems like yesterday."

Leanne met Sebastian's eyes briefly over Arthur's head. In his eyes, she saw the same silent thought: this might be Arthur's last happy birthday. Together, they would make it something special.

Sebastian popped the cork on a bottle of champagne and poured three glasses. "To the best of uncles." He lifted his glass in salute.

Leanne leaned forward, smiled and clinked her glass to his before doing the same with Arthur's.

"Happiness," she murmured. Before she could think better of it, she kissed the old man's cheek.

"This is the best present of all!" Arthur chuckled, and once again she felt the hateful blush warm her cheeks.

Sebastian abruptly turned away to start the VCR. "I think you'll enjoy this, Uncle Arthur."

"Sit down here beside me, Dr. Hunt," Arthur insisted. "You'll like this too. I remember how interested you were when I told you about my research."

The tape showed a shot of the control room juxtaposed with an exterior of the shuttle. It was just a routine mission, Sebastian explained, but each successful launch and every bit of information learned got them all closer to building a space station.

"We're way behind where we thought we'd be by now. I'm afraid I'll never get to wander the stars myself."

Leanne started. She realized that she was studying his profile; the lashes were short and thick above the sculptured bones of his face. A scientist who still felt wonder? Most of the scientists she knew were so focused on their own work they never saw beyond it. "You want to travel in space?"

He pushed the pause button, freezing an astronaut in midair. The astronaut was upside down, with a wrench in one hand and a screwdriver in the other.

"Of course." He laughed, suddenly looking as if he was on the brink of a glorious discovery. "I even volunteered for the astronaut program, but I was too late. I'm hoping I'll get picked for the space station as a scientist and that I'm not too old to go when it's finished."

He was completely serious, leaning forward intently. Arthur nodded his head in agreement.

"To man a telescope in space! Think of it, Uncle Arthur! Why, the Hubble is just the beginning. Think of what we could see. . . ."

Arthur clapped his hands delightedly. "Planets around other stars, black holes, pulsars, and more supernovas. Why, do you know, Dr. Hunt, that back when we actually identified that a supernova existed, Dr. Phillips and I were the first to . . ."

He was off, telling the story she'd patiently listened to countless times before. This time, she let the words just float around her. This time, she studied Sebastian. He concentrated on his uncle's words, throwing in an occasional fact. They didn't seem to be aware of her at all; they were lost in the world they shared. It was just as well. They wouldn't notice her studying Sebastian. The flicker of an eyebrow, the flare of a nostril, and the cleft that firmed his chin held as much wonder for her at this moment as all the stars rolled up into one supernova.

"Don't you agree, Dr. Hunt?" Arthur asked with an almost youthful eagerness.

"She's still traversing the galaxy, aren't you Doctor?"

Sebastian's cool voice brought her back to reality. She hadn't daydreamed like this, relaxed and at ease, for months. She seized on the only clue she'd heard.

"Is it possible, do you think? To travel the galaxy? To find life . . . out there?"

"That's what I'm working for," Sebastian replied gravely. "Some day, some lucky astro-traveler will awaken on a planet revolving around Eta, the double star in Cassiopeia, because of the research that I'm doing. And who knows what that traveler will find?"

He turned the recorder back on. The last portion of the tape was unedited shots of the galaxy from the deep space telescope. Sebastian excused himself to slip out. The film was just ending when he came back with a birthday cake covered with lighted candles. Arthur blew them out while Leanne and Sebastian clapped.

Leanne was glad she'd accepted their invitation. She had to learn to balance her life better. She needed more moments like this; even the chronic tightness in her neck was gone. They'd each only taken a few bites of cake when she put hers aside, noticing Arthur's pale cheeks.

"I think you need some rest." She picked up his wrist to check his pulse. "Why don't you take a little nap and I'll have the nurse wrap the rest of the cake for later."

Arthur tried to stifle a yawn behind one thin palm but failed. Sliding down on his pillows, his gaze flickered between Leanne and Sebastian. "Thank you both. This brought back so many good times. Those memories seem so close to me lately." He sighed, his eyelids drifting shut.

Wordlessly, Leanne and Sebastian walked out into the corridor, but there he stopped her.

"I want to talk to you about Arthur. There's something we need to discuss, isn't there?"

The cleft in his chin deepened when he frowned, she discovered. The determination that hardened his soft brown eyes decided her. She understood him at least well enough to know he wouldn't be put off. Perhaps now was the time, after all.

"Come to my office. We can talk there."

As soon as she sat down in her swivel chair, she saw her red paging light flashing.

"Excuse me. I need to check my messages."

He nodded and eased into a chair in front of the desk. She swiveled around, away from him.

"This is Dr. Hunt," she informed the operator. She held a pencil poised over her notebook so that she could take the messages.

A chill started in her throat, then spread through her chest, down her thighs and beyond. The pencil slid from her numb fingers. Dr. Fredricks couldn't have authorized this! A half an hour after she'd left him, Marcus Jacobs had checked himself out of the hospital. How could she have been so blind? Neither Marcus nor Joyce were thinking straight! She should have stayed. She should have been available to talk to them. Instead, she had stolen those few hours with Arthur and Sebastian.

It was her fault. She slowly replaced the receiver and rose without thinking. She'd go straight out to their house....

"Are you all right?" Sebastian asked, leaning forward in the chair, his gaze scanning her face.

"Yes. It's another patient." Taking a deep, warming breath into her paralyzed lungs, she tried to collect her thoughts. "I have to..." But what could she do tonight? A few days away from doctors, at home with his family, might be the best thing for Marcus Jacobs. Maybe then she'd be able to talk sense to him.

She swiveled the chair around and sat down again, putting her emotional response under control. Right now, she had to concentrate on the problem at hand and that was bad enough. Sebastian didn't seem the type to take this news well—he was a man of action— and there was really nothing he'd be able to do.

"As I told you yesterday, Arthur's physical therapy is going well," she began carefully. "However, he is beginning to show the first signs of Alzheimer's disease." She hadn't meant to say it so bluntly, but perhaps with a man like Sebastian that was best. "Do you know anything about it?"

"Not very much." His voice was clear and direct. She was relieved to realize he was going to discuss this calmly.

"I have a pamphlet on the condition I'd like you to read." She was thankful to have something concrete to do, some way to help. That was her job as a doctor. Too often these days there was nothing she could do but offer sympathy and comfort. She liked to fight death and hold it at bay with some kind of action.

She opened the second desk drawer to her right and lifted out the booklet on Alzheimer's disease. Resting beneath it were two blue cardboard cases. They contained Jane Doe's slides.

Chapter Three

The same chill she'd felt earlier paralyzed her. This was wrong! Those slides hadn't been here yesterday, she was certain.

"Leanne, are you all right?"

The sharp tone of his voice shocked her into action. She reached into the desk to remove the pamphlet, leaving the slides where they were. For an infinitesimal moment she considered telling Sebastian all about her vague feeling that something was wrong, but rationality stopped her. She would sound paranoid! And nothing had really happened. Perhaps she had just been careless. Whatever the case, she was a perfectly capable person, and she could handle this on her own.

"Here you are, Sebastian. Why don't you read this over and we'll discuss it tomorrow."

She couldn't meet his intense eyes for more than a fleeting glance for fear she'd give herself away. William had always drummed into her the notion that she must face patients and their families with an air of utter confidence. At this moment, she wasn't sure she could muster it, but she surely would try.

"Yes, I'll get back to you. Are you sure you're all right?"

She had no choice but to look up from where she was making a production of flipping through papers on her desk. She found him standing over her and laughed nervously. It was silly to feel so comforted by his obvious concern. Taking a deep, hopefully not too noticeable breath, she met his penetrating gaze as steadily as possible. "Yes. I just have a very serious case I still have to deal with tonight."

"Then I won't keep you." As he stepped away, the cleft in his chin deepened with a faint smile. "From what I've seen of you with my uncle, I know you'll handle whatever it is with both professionalism and compassion. Goodnight, Leanne."

His were high compliments indeed. And he was supportive. It was always surprising to find someone, particularly a stranger, in her corner. It wasn't until the door clicked shut behind him that she realized he'd called her by her first name.

She curled her fingers around the drawer handle and closed her eyes for just a second. She opened them and the drawer at the same time. The slides were still there. She wasn't seeing things! Threads of doubt wove a strong web about her. She knew positively those slides weren't in her desk yesterday. She was a detail person. She'd honed her recall skills so she could remember names and faces; she never forgot to return phone calls. In fact, her memory was so good she often remembered telephone numbers long after they were needed. Never, ever, would she have overlooked these slides if they'd been in this drawer.

Picking them up, she turned them over and over in her hands. They looked the same, they had Jane Doe's name printed clearly on the cover, but, they could be anything. There was only one way to find out.

Carla sat hunched over a microscope in the lab, as usual. When the door whooshed open, she looked up and gave Leanne a faint smile.

"Thought you were off duty." Shifting back on the high stool, she flexed her shoulders. "What's up?"

"I found the slides. Would you look at them and tell me if they're Jane Doe?"

Leanne ignored Carla's raised eyebrows and thrust the slides at her. "Please, I'd like your professional opinion."

"What is with you, Leanne?" Carla placed one slide under the scope. "Yeah, hair." Removing it, she shoved in the second slide. "Yeah, tissue. Here, see for yourself."

She leaned to one side so Leanne could bend over and adjust the focus until the slide was as clearly defined as possible. It was skin. Slowly, she removed it and placed the other slide under the lens. Hair.

Straightening, she looked into Carla's scowling face. "But how can I be sure these are actually from Jane Doe?"

"There aren't many slides like this floating around the hospital, Leanne. Besides, they're labeled. I know my job and I do it very well!" Carla retorted. "What's the deal about these damn slides? I've got to say you look like hell. Are you sick or something? Trouble with a case? Something's making you pretty jumpy."

Yes, something *was* making her jumpy. Something was off balance. Leanne just didn't know what it was yet. Until she did, she certainly wouldn't discuss it with Carla.

"If you must know, Marcus Jacobs checked himself out of the hospital." She offered the explanation to appease Carla's stiff indignation. After all, they were colleagues.

Carla gave a low whistle. "No wonder you're on edge. I did his workup. Without treatment he hasn't got a chance." Shrugging, she relaxed and crossed her legs. "Not that there's much chance with his kind of tumor. Maybe he decided against more chemo and is going to enjoy what time he's got. If so, there's not much you can do about it." The mocking eyes flicked over Leanne. "But I can tell from the look on your face you're going to try, right?"

"I'm going out to his house to talk to him." Leanne tried to answer calmly even though she was as jumpy and on edge as Carla had guessed.

"Take my advice and wait until tomorrow. Sleep on it first. You look like you could use a good eight hours."

For once, Leanne was in complete agreement with her. Maybe after a good night's sleep everything around her that seemed off would come back into balance.

She lay awake for what seemed like hours formulating arguments to present to Marcus. Finally, with the sheets tangled around her, she drifted into a light sleep. Jane Doe's slides flitted through her dreams, disappearing and reappearing in the most unlikely places. Eventually, they grew to gigantic proportions, filling her office and forcing her out into the hospital corridor. Gurneys came flying at her from every direction, turning her around and around until she lost her way. She fought through an unending maze of hallways, but never made any progress. A door opened and she rushed toward it, tumbling headlong in the process.

Disembodied faces laughed at her. Clarence Pickerell blinked his heavy-lidded eyes as he had in the mortuary hallway. Others floated by, but she couldn't quite make out who they were. Familiar faces . . . was that Sheriff Sullivan? Her mailman? Finally, one face drifted close enough to solidify. Jane Doe, her mouth twisted in a grotesque parody of a smile.

When she awoke, with the alarm blaring on her nightstand, she felt as though she'd been through a war. Fighting to open her weighted eyelids, she reached automatically for the clock. It was morning and nothing seemed any clearer. But today, she vowed to forget about the vanishing and reappearing slides. She had to concentrate on helping Marcus and his family.

She arrived at the hospital earlier than usual and consciously avoided her office. She worked hard most of the day. She looked in on each of her patients and checked their charts. Arthur was sleeping and Sebastian was nowhere to be found. Although she wasn't exactly looking forward to their talk, she found to her surprise that she was anxious to see him again. She authorized Arthur's release, took care of some other details and signed out, saying that she would be at Marcus's farm if she was needed.

Leanne drove north out of Peaceful, past the Pickerell and Pickerell Funeral Home, and past the magnolia-lined drive of Shady Rest. Marcus had built his rambling clapboard home at the very edge of the Okefenokee Swamp. He'd often told her about the herons that wandered into his backyard from the wildlife refuge. At last, turning into the driveway, she could just glimpse the many glimmers of sunlight that reflected on the swampy waterway through the moss-hung trees.

She was surprised that none of Marcus's three lively sons were playing on the jungle gym at the side of the house. For such a beautiful, sunny day she felt an odd stillness around her, but perhaps that was normal here. The place was tucked away amidst the cypress trees, and hidden by the ever-present moss that swayed gently on the breeze.

She rang the bell, then took a deep breath for courage. Perhaps she should have called ahead, but she instinctively knew if she had Marcus would have refused to see her.

On the second ring, the dark, paneled door slowly opened. The last time she'd seen Joyce Jacobs her face had been grief-stricken, her eyes washed with tears. Nothing had altered.

"Dr. Hunt, what are you doing here?" Joyce gasped, quickly rubbing her palms over her wet cheeks.

"I'm sorry to arrive unannounced, but I want to talk to you and Marcus about his treatment." Leanne could see nothing behind Joyce in the narrow foyer. "May I come in?"

Suddenly Joyce shifted, filling the doorway. "You can't see Marcus, Dr. Hunt."

Leanne did what William had taught her so well; she looked steadily and with determination into Joyce's ravished face.

"Joyce, I understand what you're going through. But denial will solve nothing. Marcus needs medical treatment. If not chemotherapy, then there are medications that could at least ease some of his pain. He needs to be under a doctor's care."

The tear-swollen eyes stared blankly back at her, then crinkled in fresh grief as Joyce slumped against the door frame. "Marcus is gone." Her head jerked up defensively as she continued. "He's seeking alternative treatment, Dr. Hunt. There's nothing more you can do for him."

Leanne felt suddenly chilled, even with patches of the Georgia sun beating down around her. "Alternative treatment? Can you tell me what kind?"

With a gasping sob, Joyce shook her head, avoiding Leanne's eyes. "The doctor prefers I don't say."

The chill spread, seeming to fill the air between them. This wasn't right. This wasn't the type of behavior Leanne had witnessed through the last year of Marcus's illness. She tried one of the many ideas she had agonized over the night before.

"Joyce, I know how much help you and the boys were to Marcus during his last rounds of treatment. How could he go off on his own?"

Nearly doubled over with weeping, Joyce continued to shake her head. "I can't say." She was whispering so low Leanne could hardly understand her.

Leanne put out a comforting hand. "How difficult this must be for you and for the boys. I'll help however I can."

Joyce took a step back. "Thanks, but there's really nothing you can do."

"Where is Marcus? At the Memorial Sloan-Kettering Cancer Center? Or the Mayo Clinic?" She studied Joyce's face carefully but there was absolutely no response. "Can you tell me who recommended the new treatment? Perhaps I could talk to—"

"No!" Joyce nodded with emphasis, her swollen eyes widening in distress. "Dr. Montague says—" Biting hard on her lower lip, she stepped back, her trembling hand on the door. "There's nothing more you can do. Please just leave us alone."

The door slammed shut in Leanne's face. She stood for a minute, just staring at it, still not quite believing any of this.

Who *was* Dr. Anthony Montague? What was he doing at her hospital? Why would he interfere with her patient? And what exactly was his tie to Shady Rest? Shady Rest. William knew Dr. Montague, and he would help her. He could explain everything.

Reluctantly, she returned to her car, determined to get to the bottom of this disturbing news. But as she drove away, she couldn't resist a glance back at the silent house. Once again, she experienced that strange sensation of being watched. And the feeling didn't go away.

It persisted until she turned into Shady Rest's familiar driveway. Only then did she feel safe. She'd always considered tiny Peaceful, Georgia, the safest place she'd ever lived. But in the last few days, that feeling of security had somehow subtly shifted. The oddest thing was that she couldn't put her finger on why.

"Leanne dear, how wonderful!" Mary clapped her hands, hurrying down the walk as Leanne stepped from the car. "William is looking for you. He has left two messages with your service. And that dishy Sebastian Kincaid said he left messages, too."

Still slightly shaken from her conversation with Joyce, Leanne blinked at Mary. Her suntanned face was haloed by fluffy blue-gray hair. "Is something wrong? Arthur?"

"No, dear, everything's wonderful! Arthur's home so we decided to have an impromptu cookout celebration. I've been on the phone all afternoon inviting people." Placing her hand on Leanne's arm, Mary drew her down one of the paths leading to the villas. "Everyone's at the pool and barbecue area. We've been hoping you'd show up to join us."

The scene around the pool reminded her of just how small Peaceful really was. Clarence Pickerell, in his habitual somber suit, stood talking to Peaceful's sheriff, Howard Sullivan. Janice and Betty, nurses from the hospital, chatted with Shady Rest residents. At the barbecue, with smoke curling above them, Anthony Montague and Carla Gregory seemed to be directing Lewis; he carefully turned chicken breasts on the grill.

"Where's William? And I don't see Sebastian." Leanne was surprised at the undeniably eager tone in her voice, but it brought a knowing smile from Mary.

"William is here somewhere. Sebastian was helping Arthur at his villa." Mary gave Leanne a prim smile. "I don't blame you for wanting to see Sebastian." She gave a little mock shiver. "He has a certain something, doesn't he? If only I was a bit younger...but there's nothing stopping you, Leanne dear." Mary gave her a small pat before bustling away to the buffet table to arrange the salads and condiments.

Leanne wondered, fleetingly and with a touch of wry humor, how Mary, so all-efficient, had lost track of William for even a moment. But no matter! Here was her chance to move in on Dr. Montague. Although she was stopped and greeted many times on her way across the yard, she was in luck. By the time she reached him, he was standing alone at the barbecue grill.

"Dr. Montague, how nice to see you again." She smiled broadly and was rewarded with his usual choppy nod.

"Hello, Dr. Hunt." He stepped to one side as if he wanted to escape quickly.

She moved, blocking his path. His thin lips settled into a stern line and his narrow eyes slitted nearly shut. Obviously she hadn't been subtle enough.

"Is there something wrong, Dr. Hunt?"

"Well, yes, I'm afraid there is." *Look them straight in the eyes with utmost confidence*. William had taught her that. "I was just out at the Jacobses. I understand you suggested alternative treatment for Marcus. I'm surprised you didn't consult me first. Can you tell me what kind of treatment Marcus is receiving and where?"

"I'm afraid I'm not at liberty to discuss this, Dr. Hunt," he answered, with the faintest hint of an apologetic smile. "The family has requested the utmost secrecy."

A deadly chill pierced her chest, lodging there. He was lying. He was looking her straight in the eyes, and he was lying to her. Joyce had insisted it was the doctor who had demanded secrecy. Leanne believed her.

"I see." She said the words as steadily as she could over the loud pounding beat of her heart. "Can you tell me if these alternative treatments have anything to do with why you're in Peaceful, Dr. Montague? You arrived here rather out of the blue, didn't you?"

"Anthony's arrival was at my invitation, Leanne."

William's unexpected interference caused her to falter. He reached a protective and reassuring arm around her, patting her shoulder. She stared up dumbly, into his smiling face.

"For several years, Anthony's been involved in a research project that is very important to geriatrics. Several of our residents are involved in his study." He shared a chuckle with a completely confident Dr. Montague. "Poor Anthony has been in and out of Peaceful so often that I suggested he just move his lab here. He did so a few months ago."

Even with William's vibrant warmth next to her, Leanne was still chilled. "Are any of my patients involved in Dr. Montague's study?"

"Why yes, they are. We're all very excited about his work." William answered her with the same enthusiasm in his voice that had always inspired her.

For the first time in their relationship, she looked into his clear eyes with something besides adoration. "I'm surprised none of them have ever mentioned this research to me. Why didn't you inform me, William?"

"Anthony, I believe Mary is trying to get your attention." William nodded dismissively and Anthony Montague made his quick escape. William gently touched Leanne's chin with two fingers. "I know this look. It's your earnest scientist look. The one that demands to be shown, not told. Have I ever failed you, Leanne?"

With William there could be no doubts. All her confusion and anger drained away and she looked up at him as she always had, with complete confidence and trust.

"No, William, you've never failed me." Her answer held a resounding affirmation, even if her words had to be forced through her throat; it felt hot with shame for that unbelievable moment of doubt.

"And I never shall." The magnificence of his smile banished the lingering effect of the frightening chill that had come over her.

"Anthony's work is revolutionary. Absolutely brilliant! Unfortunately, it is still in its infancy. I want to share it with you, Leanne. I know you'll be as enthusiastic as I am. But I want to wait until there are more concrete results. Can you be patient with me just a bit longer?" His bushy white eyebrows rose in question. Without hesitation, she nodded.

"Excellent!" He gave her a brief, tight hug, pressing a kiss on her cheek. "Now come and eat. Mary is looking rather sternly in our direction because we haven't gotten in line like the others."

Leanne stepped out of his reach and nodded. "In just a minute. You go ahead and appease Mary. I'll be right there."

He left her, striding purposefully through the crowd. His overwhelming presence had so comforted and convinced her that now she felt a little bereft. Suddenly, she was overcome by the feeling she was being watched. She spun around, but there was no one nearby except Lewis, who was totally engrossed in marinading more chicken breasts on the grill.

Leanne looked at the scene around her almost as if she were outside of it, observing. These people were her friends; some she considered family. They were the closest thing she had to one. There was a reasonable explanation for the missing slides, a reasonable explanation for what seemed to be Dr. Montague's lie, and a reasonable explanation for this overpowering feeling of being watched. On one level, she knew there must be reasonable explanations.

But on another level, she couldn't shake the feeling that now tightened around her like a web. Something or someone had altered her world. Perhaps all these people and all this seemingly innocent activity wasn't quite what she believed it to be.

What was it that was bothering her so? When she diagnosed a disease she looked for the telltale signs. There were signs here, too, but she couldn't read them. Maybe she *was* tired and overworked. Maybe she was simply overreacting in a moment of stress. But she knew she couldn't rest until she resolved it all, if only in her own mind. And she needed to do that before the thin edge of frightening desperation overwhelmed her.

"Leanne, I think I have just what you need."

Startled, she shrank back in surprise for a moment until she recognized the voice. Then she turned and looked straight into Sebastian's arrestingly handsome face.

He'd brought her a plate of food as an excuse to approach her. He wanted to shatter the mesmerizing spell that, even from across the yard, he could see William Lucus cast over her.

Why did he feel compelled to act so rashly? He didn't stop to consider that. Something about William Lucus bothered him. Maybe it was the image Leanne had painted of him as being larger than life. As a scientist, Sebastian studied the universe in its most minute detail to find answers, and sometimes the biggest problems could be solved by a tiny bit of information. So, he'd stood at the other side of the pool and watched the three doctors interact. The way William handled Leanne was almost like a lover. Perhaps they were lovers....

Something about that idea jarred him. Possibly the age difference was what he found so distasteful. But who could blame the guy? Leanne was lovely. She was as talented and dedicated as Jessica had been. Still, why did Leanne always remind him of all that old pain? She and Jessica were alike only in the merest superficial ways. For instance, in their dedication to their work. But there was a shadow of vulnerability in Leanne that had never been present in Jessica.

"Here, this is obviously what you need." Sebastian realized that Leanne had been watching him expectantly. He handed her the plate.

Blinking, she stared down at the chicken breasts, potato salad, coleslaw and corn on the cob. "I'll never be able to eat all this."

"Sure you will." He laughed, convinced she was so preoccupied that she had unwittingly lowered her guard somehow. "Come on. Believe it or not, I spy a vacant glider over there under that tree."

To his relief, she didn't protest, but kept pace with him to where the empty glider sat apart from the rest of the gathering.

The sun was setting behind the red tiled roofs and a sliver of the moon was just discernible in the twilight sky. It was darker where they sat, so they could easily watch the activity around the lighted pool area without being observed. And watching was exactly what Leanne was doing. As she nibbled from the plate of food, she stared at the crowd. What was she looking for?

In profile she looked incredibly younger, Sebastian thought. Her severe hairstyle was softened by curly wisps that lay on her forehead and brushed her small ear. He was stirred by this confirmation of her vulnerability.

"Leanne, is there something bothering you?"

He could see her jaw instantly tighten and the softly rounded chin firmed up before she laid her plate aside and turned to him with a steady, professional gaze.

"I have several challenging cases I'm concerned about. I'm sorry I wasn't more attentive. Have you read the pamphlet on Arthur's condition?"

"Yes. I understand there's no way to slow down or stop the degeneration once it begins."

"I'm sorry. But his condition can only worsen."

Nodding, Sebastian set his plate on the grass then spread his arm along the glider back. "I concluded as much after reading the material, so I'm going to spend as much time with him as I can. I'll arrange to take two or three weeks off this month and try to catch up on all we've missed."

In the dim light, her eyes flashed and were startlingly blue. "I know it will mean a great deal to him. But I'm afraid there's not much to keep you entertained in Peaceful for two or three weeks."

"Oh, I don't know. I find the sights of Peaceful particularly appealing."

He was flirting! For the first time since Jessica's death he was looking at a woman, not as a friend or a colleague, not as an object for seduction, but with affection. He was teasing her out of her mood, hoping to help her. Still, for some reason, she reminded him too much of Jessica. That fact drew him and pushed him away with equal strength. But the attraction he felt gained a slight edge when Leanne lowered her eyes like a demure schoolgirl. She was hardly giving him the stare of a hard-bitten professional.

She shifted farther away from him on the glider, away from his arm and from his obviously flirtatious statement. He made her nervous. He'd been aware of that from the beginning, but he still didn't understand why. She was a beautiful woman; she should be used to flattery and men.

"Look, Leanne, the first stars are always the brightest." Adroitly changing the subject, he looked upward, and without seeing, physically felt her relax next to him again.

"You still enjoy looking at the stars without a telescope?"

"Particularly without a telescope." He chuckled, pointing to a familiar constellation. "That's my favorite, Orion. Can you see it?"

She leaned her head back, nearly touching his outstretched arm. "No. I'm afraid I'm not very good at this. Oh! A shooting star! Did you see it?"

She turned to him with that brilliant smile she'd given Arthur and its warmth had a peculiar result. Without thinking he said, "Yes, quick, shut your eyes and make a wish."

She squeezed her eyelids tightly closed, her face set in such earnest lines he found himself leaning toward her.

"When I was in grad school, we budding astronomers had a surefire way to ensure that wishes came true." He bent over and lightly brushed her parted lips. The touch was brief enough, but it burned his mouth, sending a flame of heat to lodge in his gut.

She was staring at him with open surprise and a bit of reproof.

He met that look freely and without guilt. He was happy, almost relieved he had done it.

But something, some vague movement, pulled his eyes away from her face, past the edge of the glider. He searched the darkness behind them, careful not to let her see his concern. Casually, he moved his arm away and turned back to the gathering at the pool. He didn't know the people well enough to see who might be missing. But someone in that congenial group was watching Leanne and he sensed it was not with any kindly intent.

Chapter Four

Leanne rose slowly to her feet, and the atmosphere around them immediately lightened. Sebastian stood beside her, still searching the shadows for the invisible watcher. He was keenly aware that the kiss he'd impulsively stolen had been witnessed by someone.

"Well, it's mildly reassuring to know that budding astronomers and med students have the same mentality. Several med students tried this technique when I was in school. However, we're a little old for this kind of thing now, don't you think?"

Her mild rebuke implied he was acting like a teenager and that amused him. From what he'd seen, he doubted Leanne had ever acted like a teenager, even when she was one.

He smiled into her face. Her eyes reflected the moonlight in the yard and created a private spotlight, just for him. He reached to caress her soft lips, but instantly thought better of the impulse and covered it by gesturing toward the sky.

"I hope your wish comes true."

"I hope so, too."

The serious tone of her voice and the tightening of her full mouth jarred him back to reality. That same look was becoming quite familiar to him. It signified a withdrawal into herself and a determination to... He didn't know what her demons were or why she should even have any, but he suddenly wished he could banish that look from her face.

"We astronomers do have some other good qualities. We're very good listeners, so if you ever want to talk about what is bothering you so much...."

The widening of her eyes and her suddenly stricken look told him what he needed to know. His instincts were right. Something was worrying the beautiful Dr. Hunt. She took a step toward him as if she might be willing to confide.

"Here the two of you are!" Mary's determined cheerfulness jarred along his nerves. The mood was definitely shattered. Leanne's cool detachment slid firmly back in place.

"We've been looking everywhere for you! Sebastian, your uncle is waiting for you to take him back to his villa. And William was looking for you, Leanne." Mary's small hand patted Leanne's arm as if she were a child. "He had an important meeting, but he suggests you stay in your room at the guest villa tonight and then you can have breakfast together as usual."

What was this? Leanne flashed him a slightly wary look as if he'd telegraphed his suspicions. Was he right? Were William and Leanne lovers? Did everyone know it but him? Jealousy flared and was quickly squelched. Maybe he had been out of line with the kiss. Maybe that's what had generated all the tension he felt surrounding them. This was a tightly knit community and he was the newcomer. Perhaps he was stepping over the boundaries someone had placed around Leanne.

"Thank you, Mary. I think I will stay. I haven't been sleeping well and I don't relish the drive into town."

"The two of you just hurry along. I've got to help here. Look at this mess." Bristling with efficiency, Mary rushed away to organize the cleanup.

"She loves running things." Leanne gave Sebastian a small smile that barely curved the corners of her lips. "We'd better go. Arthur's waiting." She moved toward the pool and Sebastian followed.

"You two having a good time?" Grinning, Arthur winked at Sebastian.

Grinning back, Sebastian helped his matchmaking uncle from a lounge chair. "A great time. How are you doing?"

"Think I've had enough. Sorry to spoil the party, but I'm afraid I've overdone it a bit my first time out."

Leanne immediately assumed her professional persona. It was amazing, Sebastian thought. One minute she was vulnerable and troubled, the next she was all business. This adaptability was all too familiar for Sebastian. He'd watched Jessica change back and forth, too, until finally the professional had won out completely. But there was a difference. Even at her most professional, Leanne's genuine concern for his uncle was obvious.

"Of course you have," she was saying as she offered a supporting arm. Together they helped Arthur down the path to his villa. Leanne encouraged Arthur the whole way. "You must continue the exercise program I gave you. You'll see, every day you'll feel a bit stronger."

"You make me feel stronger just with that pretty smile," Arthur teased.

Leanne responded with a light musical laugh that echoed around them in the heavy darkness. "That's sweet of you to say, but I think a good night's sleep will help even more. Here we are." At the door, she dropped her arm and stepped back. "Rest well, Arthur."

"Hope so." Nodding, he fumbled with the lock, but shooed Sebastian away when he tried to help. "I can take care of myself. You go and walk Leanne to the guest villa like a gentleman. Go on now," he insisted with another wink.

Recognizing his uncle's eagerness, Sebastian complied. The simple gesture would give him pleasure. "I distinctly remember this tone from my childhood. Come on, Leanne, I'm walking you home."

Smiling, she waited until Arthur was safely inside before starting down the path beside Sebastian. He was touched once more by her consideration.

The night closed in around them providing a strange sense of companionship. The visitor's villa was about a hundred yards away and the path was smooth, flat and well-lit by black wrought iron gaslights that came on automatically at dusk. In their glow, Sebastian could see how the humidity curled the pale gold tendrils of hair around her cheeks. She reached up, tightening the coil at her nape. It was a nervous gesture he'd seen before.

"Do you ever wear your hair down, Leanne?" It was an impertinent question, but he couldn't take it back.

A blush crept up her face, but she showed no other feeling. Her cool, professional facade was firmly in place.

"In this heat? Never."

"I imagine it's beautiful when you let it fall free. I hope to see it that way some day." For some reason he wanted to shock her out of that professional facade, or at least see if it was possible, but she quickened her pace as if trying to escape him.

He wanted to pierce that coolness and find the woman beneath, the woman he'd glimpsed on the glider. At the end, there'd been nothing beneath Jessica's facade. For some reason, Leanne made him reach down inside himself and explore the pain of that discovery. He wasn't sure he was ready yet to face the truth. Nor was he ready for his attraction to Leanne. Could he be the kind of man who was drawn to the same woman, only with a different face, over and over again? Maybe that's why he was being so forward. He wanted to pierce the facade swiftly and find out the truth before it was too late.

She stopped in front of a small villa with two doors marked Guest where the nameplates were usually emblazoned. "Thank you, Sebastian. Perhaps I'll see you in the morning before I leave."

Her smile was polite and meant to keep him at a distance. Ignoring the warning, he reached out one arm and rested his hand on the doorjamb, trapping her with his body. She had no choice but to let her head fall back and look at him. She was now definitely on the defensive.

"I have to go to the Cape tonight. But I'll be back soon to spend some time with Arthur. I'd like to see more of you then, too."

She didn't answer; she just studied him with her clear blue eyes. Wanting to force some kind of response from her, he lifted a coil of blond hair from her neck and smoothed it behind her ear.

She stiffened at his touch. With a vigorous tilt of her chin, she tried to put as much distance between them as possible. "Sebastian, when I first met you I thought you looked amazingly like a much younger version of Arthur. Especially the eyes. I think they used to be called bedroom eyes years ago. I see you also inherited his propensity for flirting. But I believe he could still teach you a thing or two."

Admiration flared in him at her show of spirit, and it joined the warmth already stirring there. Laughing, he stepped back, freeing her. She didn't waste any time getting through the door.

"By the way, Leanne, I made a wish on that star, too," he called loudly before she could shut him out. He hoped he wasn't imagining the short musical breath of laughter that sounded before the door closed.

He retraced his steps along the winding path, but at the first gaslight set off across the grass in a shortcut to Arthur's villa. When he was completely concealed by darkness, he stopped and slipped behind a tall flowering hibiscus plant.

Someone had been watching their interchange at the door. He'd felt the same boring intensity on his back that he'd felt on the glider. Who was so interested in conversations he and Leanne might have? He was determined to find out.

Almost immediately, he heard footsteps on the path behind him. Clarence Pickerell was walking with Sheriff Sullivan, whose boisterous laugh boomed out over the lawn. The sheriff's southern drawl faded away into the night. Then across the yard, he heard Mary's voice giving orders, followed by a sarcastic response from Carla Gregory and a helpful affirmative from Lewis.

Silence. He stepped from his hiding place, continuing the shortcut to his uncle's villa. From the corner of his eye, he caught a movement and froze in the shadow of a large tree.

There could be no mistaking William Lucus's impressive voice. A moment later William came into view, the moonlight haloing his mane of pure white hair. He was speaking intently to a rapt Anthony Montague. They passed beneath the lights, and even from this distance Sebastian could see their intense expressions and hear snatches of conversation. They were saying something about a heart-lung machine and ventilator lines. After they disappeared from sight, William's voice echoed back and Sebastian definitely caught Leanne's name. Any of the people he'd seen could have been their intent watcher. Or none of them.

Finally, as he made his way to his uncle's villa, Sebastian stared up into the heavens, into the billions and billions, as a friend of his liked to say, of possibilities that made up his world. There were so many mysteries to explore and so much to do before men could reach the stars and live among them. It would be good to distance himself from that heavenly perspective and its problems for a few weeks and focus earthward. He owed too much to his uncle. He wasn't going to let guilt for his neglect keep them apart any longer. Besides, he was beginning to suspect there might be a few problems right here in Peaceful, Georgia, that required his scrutiny.

LEANNE GASPED FOR BREATH and sat up in bed, her white cotton nightgown clinging to her breasts and stomach. It had been so real! For a moment, she couldn't believe she was actually here in the guest villa and not in the strange world of her dream.

It was a dream populated by everyone she knew in Peaceful, but their faces had been strangely distorted. She'd recognized everyone this time; she wasn't sure how. They had blocked her path to William, who stood in the distance, his own face as clear and true as it had ever been. He represented safety. Off to one side, Sebastian had been a shadowy figure, apart from all that was going on.

She turned on the light, then fell back against the pillows. Analyzed calmly, the dream made perfect sense. Her subconscious was trying to deal with all the stress she was feeling. Obviously, Sebastian represented life outside of Peaceful. He wasn't really part of her world, only a dispassionate observer. The rest was her frustration at not being able to help Marcus, not understanding his sudden disappearance, and the unease she'd experienced since seeing the perfect preservation of Jane Doe's body. Everyone's reaction to her inquiries had been odd. Who had been so interested in those slides? A prickling shiver ran down her arms as she fought off the residual fear from the dream. Her alarm chose that minute to sound and she flinched involuntarily.

"Leanne, you are obviously stressed. Go jog and clear your head," she said aloud.

She was talking to herself now! With a derisive laugh, she slipped out of bed, shed her nightgown and dressed in shorts and a tank top from the small store of clothes she left in a bottom drawer.

A white mist hung over the silent grounds and seemed to muffle her footsteps. The humidity was lower at sunrise before the sun and the damp earth created their hothouse effect. She breathed in the scent of the nearby marshy lands and the exotic flowers that thrived on the grounds. She plotted a really long run, to have enough time to clear the uncomfortable thoughts from her mind.

She started off on the path between the villas, then cut across the grounds toward the trees that bordered the property. It was a little rough going, but she'd run this way before and concentrating on the ground in front of her took her mind off other things. A doe and fawn bounded across her path before she even had the chance to recognize they were there. She loved being out in nature; it restored her sense of rightness.

At the highway, she turned away from Shady Rest and traveled a completely new way. She picked up her pace. The familiar exhilaration buoyed her stride. If she hadn't been introduced to jogging by a high school track coach, she never would have realized how much strength it gave her—both mentally and physically. Without it, she never would have survived the grueling rotations of her internship and residency. Jogging had become a part of her routine, but now she only jogged when she needed to think or clear her mind.

This morning her thoughts swirled in unusual directions like the dissipating mist. She kept thinking of Sebastian's kiss and his obvious flirtatiousness. A part of her was offended—was she really so uptight?—but another part of her, admittedly a part she tried to stifle, found him appealing.

No, appealing wasn't the right word. When his lips had brushed her mouth, a jolt of heat had ripped through her body like an electrical shock. Even now, just remembering, she felt lingering remnants of that warmth. It had been so long since she'd felt honest-to-goodness sexual attraction and it was knocking her for a loop.

Smiling to herself, she stopped at the top of a gently sloping hill overlooking Shady Rest. To her right stretched Peaceful Memorial Garden Cemetery. She turned off the road and jogged along a ridge, above the tombstones. Some were old and lichened, others were sparkling white in the new sun. Just over the next rise the marble mausoleum came into view. She'd never seen it from this angle. From here it looked so much larger, overwhelming the lush vegetation surrounding it. She'd never realized how near Shady Rest's administration building it was before. She'd always approached the mausoleum by car and never suspected that the road ran along the boundary of William's property.

There were people in the parking lot area even at this early hour, but the sun was slanted at such an angle that she couldn't make out who they were or what they were doing.

She made a loop over the hill and was back on the Shady Rest grounds; she slowed her pace again. Twenty minutes later she approached the pool area and stopped. A few stretches here would be an ideal cool down.

"Leanne dear, where have you been?"

Mary's voice came out of nowhere and startled her. She jerked up and glanced around, bewildered. "Mary, where are you?"

"Here, dear, in the pool," Mary chirped. "I'm doing my morning laps." She hung on to the edge, her fluffy tinted hair covered with a swimming cap, and she squinted into the sunshine.

With a breathless little laugh, Leanne knelt beside her. "You scared me. I didn't think anyone would be up and about so early."

"Leanne dear, as you get older you need less sleep. It's one of the few consolations of aging. William's already at work in his office."

"Oh, good. I'll stop by and see him." She started to rise, then knelt down again. Unconsciously her voice lowered. "Mary, are you part of the study Dr. Montague is doing here?"

The rosy, round face, made more moonlike by the cap, tensed. "I wasn't aware you knew about Dr. Montague's study. It's very confidential."

Shocked by Mary's reaction, Leanne sought to reassure her. "Mary, I really don't know anything specific. William hasn't told—"

"Exactly!" Mary interrupted with uncharacteristic sharpness. "I'm shocked you'd think I'd be foolish enough to betray his confidence.'' With that she pushed away, gliding across the pool in a strong crawl stroke.

Staring after her, Leanne rose slowly, her breath catching in her chest. Why did Dr. Montague cause everyone—Joyce Jacobs, William, and now Mary—to act so out of character?

Swiveling around, she looked toward the administration building. William's drapes were open. Mary said he was working. Leanne simply couldn't leave it any longer. These few threads of confusion had completed the web and trapped her inside. She wouldn't be able to get out from under her fear until she could understand exactly what was going on. There had to be logical explanations for all her questions and William could provide them, just as he always had.

She set off across the yard, mindless of the perspiration that evaporated on her rapidly cooling skin. The front door to the converted mansion was still locked, so she ran around to the back entrance. The airconditioning hit her skin like a splash of ice-cold water. Her hair was falling loose from the rubber band she'd hastily pulled it through. She stopped in the foyer and finger combed it into a tight ponytail. She didn't want to look like an untidy child when she voiced her concerns to William. It was bad enough to confront him in a tank top and brief shorts that were clinging to her damp skin, but she couldn't wait any longer.

Her jogging shoes made no sound on the carpet as she climbed the stairs and walked through Mary's office to William's dark wooden doors. She pushed them open but William wasn't at his desk. In her single-minded pursuit, she didn't even think of abandoning her search. She'd decided to put these questions to William and nothing was going to stop her.

She retraced her steps and returned to the first floor reception area; she headed through the short hallway to the infirmary. It was empty, pristine in its readiness for any emergency. William was a stickler for providing the finest facilities and care for the residents of Shady Rest.

She was disappointed when she couldn't find him. She swung around to again retrace her steps and stopped. Something was different. She was certain it hadn't been like this the last time she'd visited the infirmary. Admittedly, that had been more than three months ago, but that plain door just beyond the second care station was new.

It wasn't locked. Curiosity won out. She stepped into a wide landing with broad steps that led down to a dark hallway. She hadn't known this building had a basement; she didn't think it was even possible to have basements in this part of the state. Apparently it was.

At the bottom of the stairs there were two doors. The far one stood open. She tried the first but it was locked. The second opened onto a sparsely furnished office. The blotter on the desk looked brand new. William had said Dr. Montague had recently moved his lab here. Could this office space have something to do with his study?

Shocked at her action, but driven by all the questions and doubts confusing her, she opened the top desk drawer. It contained pens, plain white paper, envelopes, and a large ring of what appeared to be new keys. Nothing in the least bit sinister. The next two drawers were empty, but the bottom file drawer was locked.

She tried two keys before the third clicked and the drawer slid open smoothly. It held only one thin manila folder. Disregarding her vague stirrings of guilt, she opened it. There were two typed pages. On the first sheet was a list of names. She scanned the names quickly and immediately recognized two as former patients, now deceased.

Florence Chambers had been her first patient in Peaceful to die. And Lois Martin had been one of her favorites. Leanne still remembered Lois's lovely red hair and her fiery spirit in the face of her heart problems. The other names weren't familiar.

In the dim light, she lifted the sheet up to examine the list more closely. A shiver ran down her damp spine when her eyes fell on Marcus Jacobs's name; it was penciled in at the bottom.

Well then, death wasn't the common thread; they certainly weren't all her patients, so she could stop feeling so paranoid. It would, however, be interesting to know what these names had in common.

She glanced cursorily at the second sheet, then came to rigid attention. "William Lucus" headed the column. Right below her own name had been neatly typed. This list contained the names of nearly everyone she knew in Peaceful. Blinking, she placed both papers side by side. Yes, Marcus Jacobs's name was on both sheets; it was penciled in on the first, and on the second, marked out with a wide black ink slash.

Footsteps sounded on the staircase. Fresh fear brought Leanne to her feet. She stuffed the folder back into the drawer, slammed it shut, and with trembling fingers, replaced the keys in the top drawer. She had no time to get out from behind the desk so she decided to brazen it out. Two thoughts pounded through her mind. Whose office was this and what could these lists mean?

"What are you doing here?"

The same rush of terror that had awakened her from her previous night's dream flooded over her when she looked up into Anthony Montague's angry face.

"I said, what are you doing in my office?" he barked out again while she stood, dumbfounded with shock, staring at him.

"I believe she is probably looking for me, aren't you, Leanne?"

The sight of William looming behind Dr. Montague released her paralyzed legs and she nearly stumbled across the office in her eagerness to reach him.

"Yes, I couldn't find you." Swallowing a hard lump at the back of her throat, she forced a smile and was warmed when William's answering one lit his eyes. "Mary said you were working, and when you weren't in your office I went looking for you."

"What were you doing behind my desk?" Dr. Montague's face hadn't altered in the slightest.

At Dr. Montague's attack, William placed a strong, protective arm around her shoulders. "Anthony, I'm sure Leanne was only curious because this is a new part of the building."

She'd been right! William would make everything normal again. Allowing herself to relax against William, she nodded. "That's exactly right. This is brand new, isn't it?"

"We've set this office up for Anthony until his lab is fully operational."

Straightening her shoulders, Leanne looked at Anthony Montague with the veneer of professionalism she'd cultivated so carefully. "I'm eager to learn more about your research. William has spoken so highly of it."

His narrow eyes shifted to William; Leanne watched as the anger slowly vanished from his face and was replaced by a bland smile.

"Thank you for your interest, Dr. Hunt."

"Now that that's settled we'll leave you to your work, Anthony. The cook has breakfast waiting for this young lady and me."

Startled, she stepped out of his comforting arms. "But how did you know I was here this early?"

"Mary told us when we saw her on the grounds. So I sent orders to the kitchen." With a farewell nod to Anthony Montague, William steered her down the hall and up the stairs. "It's pancakes you like after jogging, isn't it? Getting your carbohydrates. I'm going to join you this morning, so no backtalk, Doctor, about my cholesterol."

She laughed, more relaxed now with William and their familiar repartee. He had better cholesterol than most men half his age and they both knew it.

As promised, breakfast for two was laid out on the conference table in William's office. Settling into the leather armchair he pulled out for her, Leanne sighed. "This is wonderful. I've been so out of sorts the last few days I've hardly eaten a bite."

"Yes, I noticed at the picnic you hardly touched your food. It's this doctor's order that you eat every bit of this breakfast, young lady!"

The aroma of the hot pancakes was too much to resist so she did as she was told. William was at his best, entertaining her with his old med school stories. But when they finished, his eyes crinkled in worry.

"I think you've been working too hard lately, Leanne. Why don't you take a few days off and stay out here with us? You could use the pool, enjoy the grounds, and keep me company."

"I wish I could, but I'm too busy. You know the hospital is understaffed, even for its small size. Besides, it isn't work that's bothering me." The time had come, but now she doubted her ability to make him understand. Here with William, comfortable and at home, her fears seemed foolish, yet she couldn't quite shake them. She rose from the table and paced the floor. "It's...I don't know exactly what it is...but since I saw Jane Doe's body..."

"Leanne, I thought that issue was settled. Wasn't the body claimed and buried by the family?"

"Yes, but—"

"And isn't that what you wished for that poor soul?"

"Of course."

His questions and rational demeanor brought a rush of hot embarrassment that lodged in her chest.

"But then Marcus Jacobs checked himself out of the hospital. He's seeking an alternative treatment that Dr. Montague suggested and won't tell me anything about."

"Well, I should hope not!" William retorted with real feeling. "I would be very disappointed in Anthony if he betrayed patient-doctor confidentiality. I'm positive you would behave in the same manner if you were in his place."

She felt deeply frustrated. She couldn't seem to make anyone understand. Tears came to her eyes. She turned away rapidly, trying to hide her weakness. Behind her she heard the scrape of William's chair. Then he gently turned her to face him. There was overwhelming concern in his eyes. The concern he always exhibited when she had a problem. He cupped her warm cheeks with his strong wide hands.

"Leanne, what is this all about? Frankly I've never heard you be so irrational. You've always been the most reasonable, dedicated person I know."

She curled her fingers around his hands and slowly pulled them away from her face. For once she wasn't comforted by his words. She squeezed his hands in what was almost an apology.

"I feel better already now that you've fed me. I promise the next time you see me I'll be my old self. But, right now I have to get to the hospital and be the doctor you taught me to be."

She stood on tiptoe and hastily kissed his cheek. "I'll call you tomorrow."

"Is that a promise?"

She swung around at the doorway and smiled. "Absolutely a promise."

Still, once she was outside his office, she fled down the stairs with an energy born of fear. She was sure Dr. Anthony Montague was up to something. His lie to her about Marcus's family and those lists with names, particularly the one with her own, made her uneasy and more than a little suspicious. She didn't know exactly what she feared, but her intuition told her it was sinister. She was utterly certain about one thing. William had no idea what was really going on. Now, not only did she have to get to the bottom of this for her own peace of mind, but to protect William. Just as he'd always protected her.

Chapter Five

She made the trip to the hospital in record time. The minute she was safely behind her desk she started recreating the lists. The memory tricks she'd learned through all the long years of school made it possible to remember a great deal more than she'd thought she could. The second sheet was easiest. She tried to write the names in order, in case that might prove significant.

William Lucus. Leanne Hunt. Mary Rand. Clarence Pickerell. Carla Gregory. Marcus Jacobs. She crossed his name out. Lewis Fontain. Janice Delaney. Betty Brice. Fred Brice. Howard Sullivan. Bobby Jo Johnson. She knew all these people: doctors, nurses, the mayor, the sheriff. She could think of nothing they had in common besides the fact that they all lived in Peaceful.

Before she started to analyze, she would have to try writing out the first list. Some of those names had been completely foreign to her. She remembered the first name because it was two first names: Thomas Richard. Then had come Lawrence Haver... something. There had been another name or two she just couldn't remember anything about. Then Florence Chambers. Billy Fontain. For another name, she guessed the initials were J.C. Then came Lois Martin. And Mel... ...tt. And finally, Marcus Jacobs was penciled in.

She was fairly pleased with her lists. Side by side they didn't produce any other significant ideas. She closed her eyes, trying to picture the file. She'd opened the bottom drawer. There was one manila file. In the file were two sheets. She ran down the lists of names. Mel... Melvina! That was it. Eagerly she added the letters.

Finding her name on the second sheet had been a real shocker! Almost before she had been able to recover, she'd heard the noises and shoved the file into the drawer. Had she put the right sheet on top?

Her heart stopped for a moment. Yes, she was certain that the unfamiliar names were the last ones she saw. And, when she'd pushed the folder into the drawer, she'd seen something else. In pencil, on the flap, was the word...Ama....

A knock sounded just a second before Carla pushed Leanne's office door open. "Did you hear the news about Fredricks?" she asked, leaning against the door frame.

Hastily covering the sheets of paper with a folder, Leanne shook her head.

"He's not here anymore. He's going to concentrate on his practice down in Jacksonville. It looks like you and I will be the only full-time doctors in this hospital. If it wasn't for Shady Rest I doubt the place would even stay open."

"William wouldn't allow that to happen. You know how he feels about the availability of good health care."

"Yeah, don't we both or we wouldn't be in this backwater. Speaking of William, he called me, concerned about you." With a mocking smile, she gave Leanne a cool once-over. "I told you you looked like hell the other day. Why don't you take the afternoon off and get some rest? I'll make your rounds. The lab is slow today."

Leanne reviewed her caseload mentally. Arthur was gone, her asthma patient was ready to be released; no one else really required her presence. And she did want the opportunity to go to the town hall and discover what the records might reveal. That Carla's generosity would enable her to do that astonished her.

"Thanks, Carla. I'll take you up on the offer. I really appreciate it."

"Forget it." Shrugging, Carla sent her another mocking smirk. "I'm doing it for William. At his age he shouldn't have to worry about you." Carla's customary gruffness was somehow reassuring.

Wasting no time, Leanne drove the short distance to the tiny clapboard building that housed both the sheriff's office and the town recorder. The records room was musty and dim; an old gentleman behind the desk was nearly obscured by shadows.

"Good afternoon, I'd like to look up some information, please."

He adjusted the old-fashioned green visor on his forehead and pushed to his feet. "Name?"

"Actually, I have quite a few of them." She hoped he heard the note of apology in her voice. "We could start with Thomas Richard."

Thomas Richard was dead. He had succumbed to a massive coronary about two and a half years before she'd arrived in Peaceful. The next name was Lawrence Haver. . . .

The archivist recognized the name immediately. "Haverstrom. Fishing buddy of mine. We went back a long way, young lady. Now just what about him interests you?"

Unprepared for the question, Leanne stalled for a moment. "Well, I'm a doctor at the hospital, you know. And I'm trying to update some files that were incomplete."

It was hot and stuffy in this dark, dusty room, but shivers ran down Leanne's bare arms. Would he accept her trumped-up explanation?

"I've always thought record keepin' was a bit lax up there at the hospital. Now, you take my office here. None of them computers and keepin' things on film. I've got it all down in black and white."

She nodded enthusiastically when he paused.

"And I know where every bit of information is."

"That's wonderful." She was truly impressed and delighted that he seemed eager to help her. "I'm glad Peaceful has such a dedicated record keeper."

He didn't quite smile at her compliment, but his thin mouth did shift slightly as he went through his files for the name. Haverstrom had died of natural causes, about eighteen months before. The next name was Florence, her patient who had died about ten days after she started at the hospital. Then came Billy Fontain.

"Now, that I don't really have to look up, either. Poor kid died of leukemia about a year ago. You being a doc—I believe his brother, Lewis, had him out of state for some special treatment. But he brought him home, after all."

Was everyone on the list dead? She stood lost in thought, threads of fear weaving new patterns and pulling her in even deeper. A large book thudded down on the counter in front of her.

"Obits. If you need more, they're all in chronological order. I like my records cross-referenced. Take your time, Doc. I'll be here all day retyping these outdated forms."

He eased back into his chair and started banging away on the ancient Royal typewriter on his desk.

She was able to figure out all the names but the one she had forgotten entirely, and there were only two possibilities for that. The list was definitely chronological. There was no set pattern of death. Two people had heart attacks, two strokes, one complication from pneumonia, the boy suffered from leukemia, and both Lois and Florence had died quietly in their sleep at Shady Rest, of natural causes like Lawrence Haverstrom.

Why was Marcus's name on the list? He wasn't dead, was he? The only other name that leaped out at her was Billy's. He'd been sent away for treatment, too. Could he be connected to Dr. Montague? But he was a child and Montague's research concerned geriatrics so there couldn't be a connection. But then,

Marcus was only forty, certainly not a candidate for geriatric research, either.

What was the common thread? She went back over each obituary. Finally it dawned on her that every one of these people had been interred through Pickerell and Pickerell. Perhaps that wasn't so unusual in a town this size, but it was a starting point.

"Thank you. You've been very helpful." The man's balding head glistened in the dim light as it domed above the band of his green visor. He didn't bother to look up, only grunted a response. There was no doubt in Leanne's mind that he was glad to be rid of her distracting presence.

Such a short time ago Peaceful had been a safe, insulated place where she didn't need anything but work and her abiding friendship with William. Something had cracked the protective shell she'd formed around her world. The damage that had begun with Jane Doe exposed just how fragile it was. Perhaps that was the reason she was drawn to Sebastian Kincaid. He wasn't part of the old world, isolated and safe. He represented adventure, fun, and long-neglected romance, she admitted with an odd pang of guilt.

Stepping from the dim town hall into the bright, heavy afternoon heat, she blinked several times and adjusted her sunglasses just to be sure she wasn't mistaken. The object of her thoughts had materialized. "Sebastian, what are you doing here?"

He straightened from where he'd been leaning against her car, the sunshine brightening his brown hair to a honey color.

"I went to the hospital to see you, but Dr. Gregory said you didn't feel well and were taking the after-

noon off. It wasn't difficult to track you down. The
only things moving in this town are on the main drag.''

He smiled, deepening the cleft in his chin. ''Leanne,
shouldn't you be home resting or something?''

''Shouldn't you be back at the Cape? I thought you
left last night.''

''I did but I've been called to Washington. Since I
was coming this way, I flew to Jacksonville, rented a
car and delivered some picture albums I thought Arthur might enjoy seeing.''

Perhaps it was his thoughtfulness toward his uncle
that drew her. ''That was kind. I'm sure he's delighted. What did you want to see me about?''

''About last night,'' he said bluntly, his long mouth
curling up at one corner.

A warm flood of remembrance made her fold her
arms across her chest, as if warding off his appeal. She
couldn't handle it just now, not with everything else.
For her own satisfaction she was going to understand
those lists of names. He wasn't a part of the mystery;
his charm would have to wait.

His dark eyes held a glint of humor as if he read her
mind and would overcome her rejection. ''I'm not
going to continue our fascinating discussion about the
proper way to wish upon a star, so you can relax. We'll
take that up when we have more time. I just thought
you should know that someone was very interested in
us last night.''

She sagged against the side of the car, her knees
suddenly weak. ''What do you mean?''

''I mean someone was watching us. On the swing.
And again at the guest villa door. I hung around af-
terward to see if I could discover who, but so many

people were there that it could have been any of them. I wasn't going to mention it, but I couldn't sleep last night because I was worrying about it." His mouth tightened. "Even in a small town like this, there might be a certain fringe element that could be dangerous. I thought you should know for your own protection."

"Sebastian, are you positive about this?"

He must have heard the fear in her voice. Why else would he again trap her within the span of his arms? His hands rested on the fender on either side of her.

"You're not surprised. Someone's been threatening you. A disgruntled patient? An old lover?"

"No! Nothing like that." The metal was hot on the backs of her thighs as she pressed into the car, trying to put more room between them. He made her nervous, but not in the same way Dr. Montague did. This was more a confusion laced with an odd anticipation. "I've just felt . . . something this past week."

"Have you spoken to the sheriff about it? Perhaps you should ask for police protection."

The indefinable energy that emanated from him sparked the air around them. To ease it and her own pent-up frustration, she forced a laugh. "First of all, police protection in Peaceful means Sheriff Sullivan and I don't think he believes in intuition. Politely, of course, he'd tell me I was working too hard and imagining things. And who could blame him? There's no proof that anything's wrong here. It's just a feeling."

"Two of us with the same feeling is more than intuition. Why don't we sit down like the scientists we are and turn this into something concrete. Deal?"

It was tempting as she stared up into his dark eyes, sherry brown with the sunlight, to confide her suspicions. But he was practically a stranger and she found him too attractive for her own good.

Old habits were stronger than new feelings. She shook her head. "Thanks for your concern, but there's really nothing to discuss."

The cleft in his chin almost disappeared. He frowned, obviously not believing her. "I'll be back by Friday. Watch yourself, understand? Meanwhile, would you check on Arthur? His hip was bothering him today. Why don't you stay with him, with people you trust?"

"Of course I'll see your uncle." The rest she rejected. She trusted everyone in Peaceful, with the exception of Dr. Montague.

Straightening, she forced Sebastian to move aside as she stepped toward the car door. He opened it so swiftly she had no choice but to slip in and look up at him as he leaned toward her.

"Be careful. You don't strike me as the kind of person who imagines things. And neither am I. Do we have a deal, Leanne?"

Safety and protection. She sensed those things hovering between her and Sebastian as if they were concrete things she could touch. As much as she wanted to feel safe, she couldn't shake the reserve she'd cultivated long ago just to survive.

"I'll see you Friday, Sebastian. We'll see how we feel then."

He remained in the street. She could see him in her mirror, watching her, until she turned the corner, onto the road that led to the Pickerell and Pickerell Funeral Home.

Today there was one car in the lot. In the back, where the long, black hearse was parked, Leanne caught a glimpse of a familiar blue truck. Instead of going to the main door she walked back to where Lewis was unloading canisters from his truck.

"Hi, Lewis!"

He swung around so quickly that the metal canister fell from his hands and rolled toward her.

"Look out, Dr. Hunt!"

She stumbled back just as Lewis, with a dive, brought the bright yellow barrel to a stop. It merely brushed the side of her shoe.

"These things weigh a ton." Lewis grunted, heaving it upright. "Metal's hotter than the hinges of hell. Wouldn't have dropped it if you hadn't scared me so bad. You shouldn't sneak up on a person that way."

The reprimand from the usually jovial Lewis was on par with everything else this day. He tugged nervously on his bushy mustache. Was her sense of disquiet contagious?

"I'm sorry, Lewis." Her voice was breathy, her heart still pounding from adrenaline pumping through her veins. "I was just surprised to see you here. I knew you helped out at Shady Rest. I didn't know you worked for Pickerell and Pickerell, too."

"I'm a hard worker. You know that, Dr. Hunt." His face was red and strained; he heaved the canister onto a small, raised dock just inside the double garage doors that usually held the hearse. "I reckon I give a helpin' hand to nearly all the business folks here in Peaceful." With the back of his hand, he wiped sweat from his forehead, then peered at her with narrowed eyes. "Gotta get goin' now."

"Wait, Lewis. I just found out about your little brother, Billy. I'm really sorry."

His eyes crinkled nearly shut, the mustache curving down as his whole body drooped in sadness. "Thanks, Dr. Hunt. Billy was a great kid. My only family."

"I'm curious. Who treated Billy's leukemia? Did you ever have a specialist?"

"I did all I could. I loved that kid." He suddenly straightened, turning defensive. "I had the best docs money could get, tried everything, but in the end they just couldn't do anything." His voice trailed off. "I did the best I could...."

"I'm sure you did, Lewis. I'm just doing some reading on the new treatments and I wondered where you took him."

"It doesn't matter since the treatment didn't work." He reached for another barrel. "I've got to get back to work. You ought to be more careful around here. You really should, you know. You're liable to get yourself hurt."

He heaved the last barrel onto the dock and got in his truck. The canister looked heavy but probably wouldn't have done more than knock her over. That was nothing compared to what Lewis's cryptic words did. Her heart pounded in her throat; she stepped aside. Lewis backed up his truck and, with a grinding of gears, roared away.

Could that have been a warning? Was Lewis the watcher? But why? How could Lewis have anything to do with Jane Doe or Marcus or the lists? Besides, his name was on the second list! She was totally confused. And suddenly, a nagging thought niggled at the back of her mind, but she just couldn't capture it.

For one instant she regretted her rejection of Sebastian's help. She pushed that thought away as she retraced her steps to the front doors. Undaunted, she entered the funeral home. Clarence Pickerell was on the list, too.

She found him standing beside the entrance to the small parlor. The scent of roses hung in the air and seemed to be stirred by the piped-in organ music that played in the background. Four people surrounded an open casket and Leanne quickly averted her eyes. She had no wish to intrude on anyone's grief, but she couldn't back down now.

"Clarence, would it be possible to speak to you privately for a few minutes?" She whispered as softly as possible and he leaned toward her, nodding.

"Follow me," he mouthed, leading her back through the quiet hall to his office.

He shut the door behind her and motioned to a chair. "Please, sit down, Dr. Hunt. I have a few minutes before the official visitation begins." Settling at his desk, he slowly folded his hands on the blotter, just as he had done the last time. "How may I be of assistance?"

"I want to talk to you about funerals."

Nodding, his thin lips curved in a gentle smile. "It's very wise of you to be so farsighted. I've found it's best to make these arrangements when not under any stress, but when you're in an atmosphere of peace and calm. What do you have in mind for your interment, Dr. Hunt?"

Surprise jolted along her already frazzled nerves. "No, you misunderstand. Not my *own* funeral." Saying it brought a tightness to her chest. She saw death so often...too often. Why had she never contemplated her own? "I want to talk to you about funerals you've handled in the last three years. Beginning with Thomas Richard."

Blinking, Clarence eased back in his chair. "Dr. Hunt, is there any particular reason why you are inquiring about certain funerals?"

There wasn't a trace of hostility in his placid voice, but immediately Leanne was on the defensive. "I'm doing a research project for the hospital," she lied smoothly.

"I see. As much as I appreciate the value of research I fear I can't be of any assistance. These arrangements entail a delicate understanding between families and the establishment they choose for this last meaningful event. To betray that sacred trust, in any way, would be unforgivable. I'm sure you understand."

His blank stare indicated that he had absolutely no intention of telling her anything; she gave in gracefully, nodding in assent.

"I was sure you would." He stood, opening the door for her. "I'm sorry you're not feeling well, Dr. Hunt. This heat is quite unbearable, isn't it?"

She was next to him in the doorway and had to tilt back her head to meet his hooded eyes. "Why do you think I'm not feeling well?"

There was, unfortunately, a note of frustration in her voice and he apparently caught it. His eyelids blinked rapidly. "Why, because Dr. Gregory was making your rounds when I visited the hospital. When I inquired, she said you were ill."

"I never realized before just how small Peaceful really is," she responded as calmly as possible.

"Yes, we in Peaceful like it that way. You will, too, once you truly settle in here. Good afternoon."

His parting words haunted her. She thought she had become a part of the fabric of Peaceful in the last year. What did it take to truly settle here?

The afternoon heat was oppressive, just as Clarence had observed. It pressed down, plastering her blouse and skirt to her back. She turned up the car's air-conditioning and opened her blouse a button, focusing the air directly on the hollow between her breasts. Unconsciously, she turned left and found herself driving toward Shady Rest. Her questions had begun there this morning, but unfortunately she wasn't much further along now than she was then. She pulled over to the shoulder and took the creased lists from her purse. What was she forgetting?

Once again her heartbeat accelerated when she read her own name. How could she be included with this group? This file, the *Ama*... file. That was it! She'd gotten a glimpse of the file name when she'd hastily put the folder away.

A...m...a... It was a totally unfamiliar word. Anxious to find a dictionary, Leanne sped to the administration building and left her car right out in front. She rushed up to William's office. Neither he nor Mary were around.

She searched the shelves. They were full of volumes on medicine and geriatrics. Finally she found an abridged dictionary. It was well-worn, dated 1954. She ran her finger down the words starting *Am*. Nothing struck her. Her vague recollection was that the word was fairly long. *Ambiguous*. That wasn't the word, but it certainly fit her mood. In disgust, she put the book down and decided to keep her promise to Sebastian and check on Arthur.

She found him on his patio, leafing through a thick picture album. He looked up at her with dark, wide eyes. They were his nephew's eyes, honest eyes. Maybe on Friday she should share what little she'd learned with Sebastian, scientist to scientist. To an outside observer everything might be instantly clear. She sighed in frustration, not knowing what course of action was right. Her reaction to Sebastian was disconcerting and now it was affecting her usual logical approach to problem solving.

"Dr. Hunt, what a pleasant sight for these old eyes." Arthur patted the chair beside him. "Come and admire my family tree. There are some great pictures here of yours truly and that handsome nephew of mine."

She adjusted the cushions and peered into Arthur's face, looking for signs of distress. "How are you feeling, Arthur? I saw Sebastian in town and he said your hip was bothering you."

"Oh, this old thing!" Laughing, he slapped his right leg. "It's just this darn humidity. I'm more worried about this." He tapped his forehead with two thin fingers. "I'm getting so darn forgetful about the smallest things. That's one reason I'm getting such a kick out of these old pictures. They bring memories that are as bright and clear as your pretty face. Like this one."

Flipping a page, he pointed to a picture of himself with a very young Sebastian. Both smiled into the camera; they stood in front of a telescope.

"This was the first time I took Sebastian to my observatory. See it in his eyes? The excitement!" He tapped the picture of the young, eager face with a fingertip. "I knew right then he would follow me into astronomy. I remember this day like it was yesterday. And this one!" He laughed, going on to another photo.

So it went, page after page, as Arthur relived his past. It was a past that in the weeks ahead would become more vivid while the everyday business of living became more difficult. And Leanne could do nothing to improve his condition. How could she resign herself to this helpless feeling? This was such a waste. A fine mind like Arthur's, just slipping away to nothingness.

He turned another page and Leanne forsook her sad thoughts to enjoy another of his amusing stories. But then she saw a picture of Sebastian with his arm draped around a pretty blond girl. Something stirred in her stomach. "Who is this with Sebastian?"

"Why that's Jessica, his wife. Never noticed before how much you two look alike."

The stirring in her stomach rose until it became a heavy lump high in her throat. "Sebastian is married?"

"Yep. Quite a wedding. Straight out of grad school. Both of them at the top of their fields. She's a scientist, too. A chemist. Sharp as tacks, she and Sebastian." He nodded and beamed, pride written all over his face.

"Are you sure Sebastian and Jessica are still married?" She hated asking—that might add to his confusion—but she couldn't stop herself.

The dark Kincaid eyes widened and softened. "Of course they are. We Kincaid men don't love easily, but when we do it's once and for keeps."

He was so adamant! She nursed her wounded pride as best she could. She felt an overpowering sense of betrayal that was as illogical as it was gut-wrenching. She had actually found Sebastian charming, even appealing, and worst of all, trustworthy. To discover he was none of these things frightened her. Maybe she was overworked and overreacting to everything. Maybe Mary and Carla and William were right and she needed some time off. She needed to remember who she could really trust.

Suddenly squinting, Arthur rubbed his forehead. "There's something else about Sebastian I should tell you, Dr. Hunt, but I can't seem to put my finger on it."

Patting his hunched shoulder, she tried to reassure him. "Don't worry about it. It will come. Just give it time."

"No!" He pushed away from the table, limping slightly as he paced across the patio. "It's important! Darn memory. Why won't it come?"

Swiftly following him, she caught his wrist, noting the accelerated beat of his pulse. "Arthur, please relax. It's all right. Sleep on it. Tomorrow you'll probably remember. If not, we can ask Sebastian on Friday when he comes." Her quiet tone seemed to calm him. He nodded, squeezing her fingers with his surprisingly strong hands.

"Will you be here in the morning, Dr. Hunt? I know I'll remember by then."

"Yes, I'll see you in the morning. Why don't you rest now?"

He raised her hand to his lips, kissing it. "You're a darling. But I've told you that before, haven't I?" He chuckled. He was back to his old self. He winked before walking slowly to the sliding glass doors of his villa.

Leanne walked around to the front. The sun hung in a low red orb just over the tops of the trees and she heard voices at the pool. She started toward them, anxious to be with someone. She wanted to shake off the unexpected disappointment that had overwhelmed her when she'd learned Sebastian was married. She'd been acting foolishly because he was the first sexy man she'd met in years. Maybe she was being stupid about everything else as well.

"Leanne, where have you been? I've been worried sick!" William exclaimed, rushing toward her with long powerful strides.

"I did double duty today so you could get some rest. The least you could have done was go home and take a nap," Carla snapped simultaneously, her hands on her slim hips.

Engulfed in William's embrace, Leanne stared at them in bewilderment. "What is all this fuss about?"

"Leanne dear, I've been on the phone all afternoon trying to locate you. We all know you haven't been yourself. We've been worried sick," Mary scolded, her face stern with disapproval.

Only Anthony Montague stood aside, saying nothing, merely observing.

"I just ran some errands. I ran into Sebastian Kincaid in town and—"

"I thought he went back to the Cape. What is he doing here again so soon?" William asked. His voice dropped to its habitual calm tone.

"He was on his way to Washington and stopped to bring Arthur some things. He asked me to check on his uncle. That's where I've been for the past hour and a half, looking at old photos with Arthur."

"How is he doing, Leanne?"

All she had to do was give her head a small shake and William understood. His eyes grieved.

"It's progressing more rapidly than we thought, isn't it?"

"I'm afraid so. When Sebastian returns on Friday, I'll have to tell him."

"Well, it isn't over yet. We'll do everything in our power to keep Arthur's fine mind as sharp as possible for as long as possible. Right, doctors?" he urged, with the same enthusiasm that had fired her imagination in med school.

"Of course we will, William. But if Leanne makes herself sick, which she is obviously doing, she won't be able to help anyone. I suggest you order her to stay in the guest villa tonight. At least that way you can keep an eye on her."

Carla's insistence rankled. But it did make sense. She'd already decided she needed some time off.

"I'll get the villa ready and order the cook to bring a tray so you can have it in bed."

"No, really..." Leanne's protest was wasted on Mary who ignored it and dashed toward the kitchen.

"William, please—"

"I agree with Carla," he interrupted. He smiled his wonderful smile. "You are totally outnumbered. I told you this morning you should stay here and rest. Now I insist. At least until morning."

Sebastian had warned her that someone had been watching them here, but she allowed their concern to lull her into a sense of security. After all, she now knew Sebastian wasn't to be trusted.

"Okay, you win." She laughed, holding her palms up in defeat. "I confess I'm so tired I could go to bed right now."

"And that's exactly where you're going, young lady." Holding her hand in a warm grip, William pulled her toward the villa. She glanced back once and discovered that Dr. Montague had already slipped away.

After a long, hot shower she found a tray beside the turned-down bed, with a note from William saying he'd see her for another breakfast of pancakes. Smiling, she leaned back on the pillows and picked at the chicken and rice. It felt good to be pampered, to know everyone was so concerned about her. Now, if she could just put all her questions to rest! She finished a tall glass of ice-cold tea and put the tray on the dresser.

Stress could play tricks with your mind; she knew that. She'd just never believed that she would be so susceptible to stress. Her utter lack of good judgment was uncharacteristic. Maybe she should get a good night's sleep and forget this craziness. It had her running all over town asking questions. But the file *did* exist. There *were* two lists. What did they mean?

That was her last thought. An incredible wave of fatigue swept over her and although she tried, she couldn't fight its pull.

AFTER HIS SHOWER Sebastian wrapped a towel around his waist and sprawled on the bed. He opened his briefcase and took out the file on Dr. William Lucus. It was thick and complete. Sometimes it helped to have friends in high places who could act quickly and efficiently when you called in favors. Slowly, as he went over each sheet of facts, Sebastian's mood grew grimmer. Dr. Lucus was impressive, unimpeachable, and a pioneer in geriatrics. His Shady Rest was a model retirement community with an impeccable reputation.

Was it just him? Or did he doubt Lucus because something hot and low twisted in his own gut every time he saw the guy touch Leanne? And Lucus certainly did touch her more often than necessary. Jealousy had never been one of Sebastian's vices. He didn't ever remember feeling it with Jessica, not even about her work, which had been her true passion. And which had destroyed her.

Flipping the file closed, Sebastian fell back on the pillows and stared at the ceiling. What was it about that town that made him uneasy? Certainly the feeling that someone had him under surveillance was a factor, but there was more. Maybe it all stemmed from his feelings about the lovely Dr. Hunt. When he had rushed to Peaceful, he'd had no intentions of concentrating on anything but a joyful reunion with his long-lost uncle. How could he have even suspected he'd meet a woman who, after all this time, stirred something dormant inside him? Soon enough he'd be back there to explore everything he was feeling. Anticipation and the sense that Leanne was in danger made the week loom frustratingly long before him.

Chapter Six

Struggling, her mind beating against the persistent wall of oblivion, Leanne forced her eyelids open. Something had brought her back from the dreamless sleep. Flinging the sheet off, she grabbed her short cotton robe and belted it as she padded to the window. Her eyes felt so heavy! She blinked, trying to clear her vision. Finally she could focus. She could just make out movements, across the yard near Arthur's villa, where every light was blazing. Something was wrong!

She was out her door immediately, running across the cool damp grass in her bare feet, her head pounding with a dull ache. The sliding glass patio doors were slightly apart and she inched through.

"I'll call the Cape and get Sebastian's number in Washington," Leanne heard Mary sob. The older woman rushed out the front door without seeing Leanne.

William turned, his face haggard with age lines she seldom glimpsed. "Leanne. You heard!"

She felt herself swaying but refused to give in to the strange light-headedness. "Arthur's dead, isn't he?"

"He passed away in his sleep. Anthony saw his lights, came to investigate and found him. Leanne!"

He caught her as she fell and held her tightly against his chest. His hand smoothed her hair where it hung down her back.

"Leanne, I know how hard it is for you to accept death. That's why you're such a good doctor. But you must also know when to let go."

His words barely penetrated her sleep-dazed mind. All she could think about was the mysterious file. Would Arthur's name now be eliminated by a wide slash of ink on one sheet, then be penciled in on the list of death? For a fraction of time her mind went completely blank. William's continuing words of comfort were a jumble she couldn't quite make out.

She stepped back and stared up at William helplessly. Arthur was gone. How would Sebastian deal with it? How would she? He was such a dear old gentleman, and he had recovered so well from his surgery. It was hard to believe he was really gone forever.

William's strong face suddenly softened in grief. "Such a pity. Arthur was a brilliant mind." Then he seemed to pull himself together. "Leanne, you're exhausted. I'm taking you back to your villa. I'll handle everything."

A pounding ache blurred her vision and dulled her senses but she tried to protest. She wanted to help, but it seemed to be all she could do to even get back to her villa. Even though she tried, concentrating with every shred of strength to fight the encroaching lethargy, she couldn't keep her eyes open once her head hit the pillow.

SEBASTIAN SLOWLY replaced the phone receiver in its cradle. How could it be true? When he'd left Arthur only hours ago, he'd been happily poring through the family picture album. How could he be gone, just like that?

Running his fingers through his hair, Sebastian paced the hotel room carpet. He stared out at the lights of Washington that twinkled below him, letting his thoughts wallow in vain regrets. He should have stayed with his uncle. He should have taken his holiday immediately, not waited until Friday. And they'd had such a short time together, but at least they'd had the last week. Thank God Arthur had contacted him or he might have died alone, estranged from his family... like Jessica.

Refusing to dwell on those old wounds, Sebastian reached for the phone. He would cancel his meetings and take some time off immediately. NASA could carry on without him. But he had the strangest premonition that Leanne might not. For now, he would dwell on the positive. Arthur had lived a long and productive life and Sebastian hoped he had added some small joy to it. All he could do for his uncle now was to straighten out his affairs. And perhaps, at last, face some problems of his own.

WHY DID HER HEAD feel as though it was twice its normal size and full of cotton wool? Blinking, Leanne stared up at the cream ceiling. Patterns of sunlight filtered in through the closed blinds. Slowly, rational thought entered her mind. She was in the guest villa and last night Arthur had died.

She sat up quickly and the blood rushed from her head. Dizziness blurred her vision, but she stiffened her spine, fighting to stay erect. She knew she was stressed out and exhausted, but she hadn't realized how much. She must overcome it; she had one important thing to do before she saw anyone. Taking deep breaths, determined to rid herself of the last fuzzy fatigue, Leanne slipped into shorts and a top. Glancing at her watch, she was surprised it was so late. She gauged her time. She didn't have to report to the hospital until one.

Outside, the heat hit her, wrapping around her like a second skin. She walked slowly across the yard to the administration building. In case anyone watched her, she wanted to appear quite casual. She didn't dare look around.

The front entrance was open and the cool air whispering along her shoulders brought a shiver. No one was in the foyer or in the infirmary when Leanne slowly opened the door. She was intent on one objective only, exploring the small, sparsely furnished office in the basement. She needed to look at the file again, to discover if Arthur's name had changed lists.

The door inside the infirmary was tightly locked. The knob wouldn't even turn in her hand. Desperate, she knocked loud and long. She didn't care who was down there. Even if she couldn't get to the file right away, she had questions that demanded answers. Maybe Montague would come. Maybe he would give something away. She wanted anything that might give her a clue as to what was going on here. Because something was definitely wrong. Those same instincts that made her a good diagnostician were opening up her mind to a myriad of possibilities. None of them were good.

"Leanne, dear, I can hear you pounding all the way upstairs! Whatever are you doing?"

Leanne swung around, anger and pure burning frustration scorching her throat.

"I'm sorry I disturbed you, Mary." Leanne tried to speak normally to alleviate Mary's blinking bewilderment. "I need to speak to William or Dr. Montague and I thought they might be down in his office."

"No, dear. Anthony signed the death certificate and went into town to file it." Sniffing, Mary dabbed at her eyes with a lace handkerchief. "And William is making final arrangements for Arthur."

At Pickerell and Pickerell, just like the others, Leanne knew. The pattern was repeating itself. "I'll try to catch him at the funeral home before I report to the hospital."

Leanne was already moving across the room, but Mary put out a hand, halting her. "William would have my head if I let you run off without a proper meal. You look like you need one. Why don't you go back to the guest villa, shower and change? I'll bring you a tray."

In too much of a hurry to argue, Leanne nodded. "All right. But I have to leave in an hour."

As the hot water streamed over her head, Leanne felt a measure of sanity return. Why had she gone off so half-cocked earlier? That wasn't like her at all. If anyone but Mary had discovered her trying to get down to Montague's office she could have been in real trouble. And what good would it do now, anyway?

She couldn't bring Arthur back. Tears mingled with the shower spray. She'd really miss him. He'd started opening her heart with his gentle flirtation and courtly ways. In all honesty, she had to admit that his nephew had played an even larger role in that department.

But of course, all that had to be forgotten now. He was married. Now, yesterday's anger and distrust were replaced by an odd yearning. Despite the pictures and Arthur's words, she still wanted to trust Sebastian. It might not be smart, but her feelings were her feelings. And many things depended on her intuition; there was no denying that. Still, she was as confused about Sebastian as she was about Montague and the rest. And she couldn't understand why she was so tired.

Yawning, she wrapped her hair in a towel and pulled on her robe. True to her word, Mary stood primly beside a tray; it was on the bedside chest when Leanne came out of the bathroom.

"Here you are, dear. I brought some lunch. I'm going to stay and watch you eat every bite. We've all been worried about you." Mary tempered her scolding with a motherly smile. "Sit right here on the bed."

With a rueful glance, Leanne did as she was told. Actually, the chicken salad was delicious and satisfied a gnawing emptiness in her stomach. "This is wonderful!"

Her praise was rewarded with a beaming smile. Mary patted a curl near Leanne's forehead. "Thank you, dear. I gave the recipe to the cook myself. Now, drink all this iced tea down. You need fluids in this heat."

Parched, Leanne drained the glass. Mary was right. She probably was slightly dehydrated; that's why the remnants of fatigue still clung tenaciously to the edge of her consciousness.

Yawning again, she laughed. "I can't believe this, but I swear I could take another nap."

"Why don't you, dear? You've plenty of time." With one small hand, Mary urged her back on the pillows and suddenly Leanne was too sleepy to resist.

"Okay, just for a little while." Stifling yet another yawn, she looked up with weighted eyelids into Mary's face. "Promise me you'll wake me in half an hour."

"Of course, dear, of course."

Of course Mary would. She was conscientious and efficient. Leanne sighed in relief, allowing her eyes to close. She was so lucky to have such a concerned friend to take good care of her.

"SEBASTIAN, I can't tell you how sorry we all are. Arthur was a brilliant scientist. His contributions to astronomy were immeasurable, and his personal friendship was a source of great joy to me. He left very specific instructions, which I carried out today. I left a copy of his will for you on the desk."

William's impressive voice resonated through the villa's living room. It bothered Sebastian, but he wrote that off to jet lag and concern. He'd thought Leanne would be here. As soon as he'd taken care of his responsibilities, he would find her. Whatever it took, he was determined to find out the cause of fear he had seen in her clear blue eyes.

"Thank you, William. I appreciate everything you've done, but I'll handle it from now on." He tried to keep his voice cordial, but he resented the authority William had usurped. "I'll go out to the funeral home to say goodbye to my uncle and arrange a small grave-side service. I think that would be best.''

"But my dear boy, you don't understand. All that's been taken care of. I'm sorry. If I had realized . . . but in these last few years Arthur had come to depend on me so completely that I just went ahead . . .''

Something in William's voice caused Sebastian to turn and study the older man. He stood proudly erect in front of an electric fireplace, his arms folded behind his back. He must be in his late sixties or early seventies, Sebastian thought, especially given his amazing list of credentials, but he looked years younger. Why wasn't he more impressed with Dr. William Lucus? Was it really something he had sensed about the doctor's relationship with Leanne that turned him off to all the undeniably good qualities Lucus possessed?

"What exactly are you saying?'' Sebastian finally asked.

"I went ahead and had the body cremated. It was Arthur's expressed wish.'' William attempted to forestall the gathering rage.

"You did what! Before I could see him? My God, man. It hasn't been twenty-four hours!''

"I'm sorry, Sebastian. In my grief, my only thought was to carry out Arthur's wishes as soon as possible. I've already scheduled a memorial service at Pickerell and Pickerell tomorrow morning.''

Regret and sorrow were forgotten in the burning resentment Sebastian felt. This presumptuous—! He would never have the chance to say goodbye properly. Pride drove him to the desk. He scanned the documents. "There's no provision for cremation here." He stated it boldly, in a direct challenge to William's authority.

"No. His wishes were all expressed verbally and to me personally."

He had to give the doctor credit; he wasn't letting anything rattle him. Suddenly anxious to be alone, to examine the unthinkable—that his uncle's death could somehow be connected to Leanne's fear—Sebastian changed the subject.

"By the way, does Dr. Hunt know about Uncle Arthur? I tried the hospital, but they said she wasn't in today. She's not answering her home number, either."

"Leanne has been notified. She was as upset as we all are. I'm sure she'll be in touch with you soon. Leanne is deeply involved with her work and her patients, as I'm sure you've seen. Now I know you'd like to get some rest. I'll see you in the morning." He clasped Sebastian's shoulder briefly before striding with stately dignity out the front door.

The sun was hovering just above the trees, leaving the room in shadows. Sebastian watched William's progress across the yard. Was it his imagination or had the good doctor deliberately avoided telling him where Leanne was? *Deeply involved in her work.* Yes, Sebastian had seen that. Jessica had been the same way and it had killed her. The similarities were only superficial, he reminded himself. He had no reason to be filled with a sense of foreboding. Jessica had foolishly persisted with research that everyone had told her was too volatile. Was Leanne doing the same thing— bucking the establishment in this quiet backwater?

Picking up the phone, he dialed Leanne's number again. He felt his pulse begin to race at the sound of her voice on a recording. Where was the beautiful Dr. Hunt?

SHE OPENED HER EYES to such blackness she could still have been in peaceful oblivion. Then objects began to slowly take shape, separating from the darkness to become the familiar furniture in the guest villa at Shady Rest. Her numbing fatigue was gone; she felt rested in a way she hadn't for weeks. The only thing remaining was a slight headache.

Then she realized it shouldn't be dark out. Where was Mary? She looked around in a state of panic. Scrambling up, she fumbled for the bedside light, squinting in the sudden glare as she tried to read her watch. She'd slept the entire day.

Then she saw the note. Mary begged her forgiveness, but Leanne had been sleeping so peacefully that Mary hadn't had the heart to wake her. When she'd told William, he'd insisted Leanne should rest. He had taken her car into town to perform her duties at the hospital himself. When Leanne was ready to leave, she should call and someone would drive her in. The PS curled Leanne's mouth into a smile. Mary was sure the hospital would be thrilled to have one of the founders and a distinguished physician like William actually doing rounds.

Leanne couldn't help chuckling at Mary's adoration of William. It wasn't new. Everyone who knew him felt the same way. He was such a compassionate man. It was so considerate to take time out of his busy schedule to do this for her. She must resign herself to the fact that her friends had recognized her complete state of exhaustion when she couldn't. She had to admit she felt a million times better than she had earlier.

Then she remembered Arthur. Overwhelming sadness engulfed her anew. On impulse, she went to the window. Slanting the blinds open to the night, she could see across the yard; its placid beauty was somehow soothing.

There was a light on in Arthur's villa. Who could be there at this hour? She was determined to find out. Now that she was well-rested her mind was alert to the threads of clues she'd gathered, and she was ready to explore them until she reached a conclusion.

She dressed in the last of the clean clothes that William had insisted she leave at Shady Rest for her frequent visits: a simple turquoise cotton skirt and matching short-sleeved sweater. She pulled her hair, which had unfortunately dried in unruly waves, into a ponytail. She hunted for a flashlight, then set off across the lawn.

SEBASTIAN HUNG UP the phone without leaving another message on Leanne's recorder. He had already left six. When he turned and saw her pulling open the patio door, his relief far outweighed any shock. In two strides he crossed the distance between them. "Where have you been? I've been leaving messages for you all over town."

She raised her delicate brows at the tone of his voice and deliberately stepped past him into the living room. "I wasn't feeling well so I took a day off to rest. I'm sorry I wasn't available for you."

Her cool, detached air was so firmly back in place that Sebastian actually retreated a step. He'd thought they'd made a little progress, but apparently he'd been wrong.

"I'm deeply sorry about your uncle, Sebastian. It was a shock to all of us."

She was holding herself firmly in check, on the defensive with him. He'd have to fight his way through it. Whether she wanted his help or not, she was going to get it! He had to understand what was going on here and satisfy his suspicion that Arthur's death might have something to do with whatever continued to trouble her.

"Leanne, has something new happened? What's the matter with you?" He moved toward her, hoping to break down the barrier but she, in turn, retreated. "You said you'd share it with me when I got back. Well, here I am. I want to help you, Leanne. I wish you would trust me."

How had he once thought her blue eyes cool? Now they shot him such a scorching look of reproach that he was struck motionless.

"This is hardly the time for that." Her hands made vague dismissing motions in the air before she continued in the same even tone, "Will any other family members be attending the service?"

Her voice was at odds with a certain hardness in her eyes, a look he'd never seen before. Her cool, crisp question demanded an answer.

"According to Arthur's instructions, he wanted an immediate cremation and only a brief memorial service. William has scheduled it for tomorrow. Unfortunately, neither my parents nor my sisters can arrive in time.''

''And your wife, Jessica. Will she be attending with you?''

Shock froze his face muscles, but he managed somehow to answer. ''My wife has been dead for four years, Leanne.''

Color flooded her pale cheeks. Her eyes widened and her lips parted as she slowly lowered herself onto a tweed sofa.

''I'm sorry. Arthur—Arthur apparently wasn't aware of her death.''

''I told him a few days ago. Obviously he forgot.''

Something in her face, a crack in the cool, detached facade, drew him to the sofa. He sat beside her. Rubbing one temple with her long, slim fingers, she looked at him with a glimmer of something besides caution for the first time that night.

''Sebastian, I apologize. I don't have any excuse for my behavior. Your uncle's condition was such I should have made other inquiries before jumping to conclusions. My only excuse is this nagging headache.''

''Are you sick?'' His voice was sharp with concern.

''No, it's only a little bit of a headache now. I think it might be from too much sleep. I've literally slept the last two days away in the guest villa.''

''You've been here all the time?'' Alarm bells went off in his head. He was right in his first assumption about William. He couldn't shake that vague sense that something was unusual in William's relationship with Leanne. ''I asked for you, but no one told me you were here.''

She shook her head, faint color still marking her high cheekbones. "William and all the rest are very protective of me. Too much so sometimes. Especially Mary. She's been spoon-feeding me in bed all day. I'm sorry you were so worried, but I did see Arthur just a few hours before he passed away." Her smile was sweet and it warmed him the way it must have his uncle. "He was so happy, Sebastian. Your album brought back great memories. We spent almost two hours together going through the pictures."

"That's when you saw Jessica and he told you we were married?"

"Yes." She glanced down, then suddenly lifted her head and looked openly into his eyes. "I resemble your late wife, don't I, Sebastian?"

Her simple question was overwhelming. It raised a new perspective and feelings he wasn't quite sure of. A knot formed in his stomach. Instinct demanded that he pull her into his arms. Instead he sat quietly, meeting her questioning eyes with complete honesty. "Superficially you're alike. You're both tall and fair and . . . beautiful."

That compliment caused a slow flush to rise from her throat but she continued to study him with clear eyes.

"Jessica was a dedicated professional. A pioneer in her field. She was working on an alternate fuel. There was an accident at her lab. . . ." His voice trailed off. He was never able to think about this without a lingering twinge of guilt. "I wasn't there when it happened. There was nothing I could do to help her."

An instinct too powerful to fight brought his hand up to cup her chin. "I can't easily accept that, the way you have trouble accepting the loss of a patient.'' His thumb rotated gently against the fullness of her lower lip. ''We're the ones who are alike, Leanne.''

She sprang to her feet and smoothed down her short skirt nervously. ''I apologize for bringing it up. The memory of her death is obviously painful for you. Especially now, with Arthur's unexpected passing. Is there anything I can do to help?''

He rose to face her, giving himself that little time to control the emotions she wasn't able to deal with, the feeling that sprang up unbidden between the two of them.

''Would you go to the memorial service with me tomorrow morning? Since you're staying here with William, I could meet you and drive you to the Pickerell and Pickerell Chapel.''

A slightly wary, or was it puzzled, look clouded her face. He'd noticed it before, especially when someone was making assumptions about her relationship with William. It confused him. Why would she run away from the feelings budding between them if she wasn't involved with someone else?

A shy smile transformed her face. ''Actually, I'm not staying here tonight.'' She was quick to set him straight. ''As soon as I find Mary, I'm getting a ride into town. But I'd be happy to attend the service with you. I can meet you there.''

''Fine.'' Relief loosened the tight knot in his gut. ''I'll drive you home tonight and pick you up in the morning.''

She hesitated just a second, then nodded. ''All right. Give me a few minutes to get my things from the guest villa.''

Pleasure at her compliance dissolved the tight knot of tension in his stomach. Leanne wasn't completely comfortable in his company—he'd recognized that from the outset—but at least she wasn't putting up any more barriers.

Sebastian waited on the porch while Leanne called Mary and gathered her clothes. Suddenly, he was struck again with that sensation of being watched. Casually, he surveyed the open grounds around the villa. Nothing stirred in the hushed night; it was so heavy with heat that the very air seemed tranquilized by it.

The Georgia sky was overcast. The ribbon of road was visible only because of his car lights as they pulled away from Shady Rest. There was nothing but black emptiness in his rearview mirror on the drive into town. Still, he couldn't shake the feeling that someone was very interested in his and Leanne's whereabouts.

He turned onto her quiet street. There was nothing suspicious: no cars, no hiding places, no one waiting at her door, as he had half-conjectured there might be. Finally, he relaxed his shoulders. Maybe he was wrong after all.

He walked her up to the covered porch of her bungalow. The moon broke through the clouds, lengthening the shadows around them. They stood for a moment, not speaking. He knew he didn't want to say good-night.

A dog barked a few yards away and instinctively Sebastian turned toward the sound. He saw a flash of white behind a pine tree in the neighboring yard. A rush of adrenaline hit him like a kick in the stomach.

His instincts *had* been right all along. He trapped Leanne against the front door so she was pressed firmly into the wood. Without warning, he brushed her lips with his mouth and she gasped.

"There are no shooting stars tonight!"

"Speak for yourself.' He laughed loudly for the benefit of their listener. Resisting the push of her palms against his chest, he leaned into her, dragging his mouth across her cheek. "There's someone watching us. Just go along with whatever I do." He did little more than breathe the words into the shell of her ear, but instantly she understood.

Her wide, blue eyes blazed up at him, but he pulled her into his arms and pressed his mouth to her trembling lips, in a promise of safety.

Even with his muscles bunched in readiness to bound down the steps and take their lulled watcher by surprise, desire stirred his senses at the taste and feel of her in his arms. Resisting the urge to prolong that feeling, he ripped himself away and took the steps in one leap. He heard the intruder crashing through the bushes ahead of him. The moon disappeared abruptly, and under the veil of darkness the sound echoed back, almost as if two people were fleeing.

When he was halfway through the backyard of the last house on the block, Sebastian came to a gasping halt. He turned on his heels and raced back the way he'd come, fear beating in his throat. What if there *were* two people and he'd left Leanne alone, unprotected? His heart pounded painfully against his ribs. He came to a swaying stop on the steps. He saw that she was safe, standing in the open doorway.

"Sebastian, are you all right? What happened?"

He brushed her questions aside, shut the front door, turned the lock, and headed to the phone on the desk. "I think there might have been two of them. I'm calling the sheriff."

"No, wait." She grabbed his wrist and he dropped the receiver back into its cradle.

"Wait for what? This is at least the third, maybe fourth time I've sensed someone watching us."

"Sensed, Sebastian. This is the first time we have any actual proof. And this might have just been kids. Peaceful is a small town. I don't want to make trouble for some poor parents by involving the sheriff."

She wasn't telling him everything. Now that the cool facade was stripped away by her vulnerability, her face mirrored her emotions.

"Then what do you suggest we do?" he asked, holding in his frustration by folding his arms across his chest.

"I'm going to be on my guard and you should be, too. We'll wait to see what happens. I'm not afraid. I've been on my own a long time, Sebastian. I can take care of myself."

No, it wasn't fear for herself he saw in her eyes. Just who did she think she was protecting? She should be afraid. Jessica should have been afraid. If he'd been closer to Jessica he would have stopped her from taking the risks, and from performing that final experiment that took her life. Maybe that failure was what drove his need to protect Leanne now.

"I'm sure you can take care of yourself, Leanne. But for my own peace of mind, would you let me check all the windows and doors for you?" Somehow he managed to keep an even tone in his voice even though he was consumed with frustration. Something was wrong here.

She knew it, too, but didn't trust him enough to share her doubts. All he could do was hope that eventually she would. He prowled through the house, checking all the double-hung windows in the combination living-dining room and the small, high window over the kitchen sink. He stopped to double lock the back door. The updated bathroom had only one narrow, frosted glass window between the shower stall and the mirrored vanity.

Across the hall, Leanne's bedroom was at odds with the rest of the tidy bungalow. Where the other rooms were stark and functional, her bedroom was soft and warm, with a matching rose and cream floral print comforter and drapes. The white wrought iron bed held small lace pillows, one shaped like a heart.

Leanne had quietly followed him from room to room, but here she seemed uncomfortable, and urged him along. "See, all the windows are locked securely." As quickly as she could, she flipped off the light, ushering him out. "Thank you for your concern, Sebastian."

She wasn't ready for him to see this side of her nature, he guessed, no more than she was ready to share what she knew with him. He stopped obstinately and lifted her chin with his fingers. It was some consolation that she allowed this familiarity again. Perhaps she had been as affected by their kiss as he had.

"Leanne, you're involved in something you shouldn't be. If something or someone is threatening you, I want you to think very carefully about sharing it with me. If you can't tell the authorities, you can tell me. It'll be all right." Her eyelashes flickered. For a heartbeat, he thought she'd give in.

She shook her head. "Thank you for your concern, but I'm sure it's nothing like that." Stepping back, she freed herself.

He let his hand fall to his side. "All right then, I'll see you in the morning. Pickerell is on the last road inside the city limits, and I turn right as I come from Shady Rest."

"Yes. Good night, Sebastian."

He waited on the front porch until he heard the bolt fall into place. That would have to do for tonight. But tomorrow he had every intention of launching his campaign to convince her she wasn't alone in this; she could trust him. He wasn't going to fail her as he'd failed Jessica.

The air in her small living room shimmered with Sebastian's energy. What fear made her insides tremble so? Was it the effect Sebastian had on her? She had been so overwhelmingly relieved that he wasn't married. She felt stupid for leaping to the worst possible conclusion and so vulnerable in the face of her emotions. She almost trusted him. If it was only herself involved, she really believed she'd share all she knew with him. But, it wasn't just her.

She rested her forehead against the wooden door, his words playing over and over in her mind. She was going to have to trust him. He'd given her every reason to. He was the only one who accepted her fears and didn't try to explain away her questions. She'd make him understand that William needed protection, too. There was no one else to turn to. And, strangely, she felt relieved to have someone with whom she could share the burden.

Dr. Montague knew she suspected him. Perhaps he even knew she'd been through his files. There was no doubt he was involved in something strange. He always seemed to be lurking around just at the times when things happened. She couldn't seem to let go of his refusal to discuss Marcus's treatment with her, despite William's reassurance. But she hadn't the faintest idea how Montague could be tied to her Jane Doe and the missing slides.

Still, William trusted him. And whatever Montague was doing in his so-called research could implicate William. She couldn't allow that to happen. So she couldn't tell Sebastian, after all. He was too anxious to involve the police.

No, the only course open to her was to investigate by herself, lay all the facts in front of William, then let him handle the matter as he saw fit. That way he could disassociate himself from Montague's wrongdoings. That decided, she firmly pushed Sebastian from her mind. She had facts to gather.

She dialed a number and waited while it rang— once, twice. On the fourth ring it was picked up.

"Jacobs's residence. Joyce speaking."

"Hello, Joyce. It's Dr. Leanne Hunt."

Even across the wire Leanne had an impression of sudden tension.

"Hello, Dr. Hunt. How can I help you?" Joyce wasn't any better at disguising her feelings now than she was in person.

"I'm calling to find out if you've heard from Marcus. How are his treatments going?"

"Marcus's treatments are going as well as can be expected," she answered after a slight hesitation.

"I'm glad to hear that. Will you be seeing him anytime soon?" She held her breath and waited for the answer.

"Actually I . . . saw him yesterday."

Her words brought a rush of relief. "You did? Wonderful!"

Marcus was alive; it wasn't necessarily a list of deaths, then. There must be another common thread she hadn't discovered. "When you see him again please give him my best."

"I will. Thank you."

The phone went dead in her hand and she replaced it slowly. At least this one fear weighing on her could be lifted. Marcus was alive. There was something else everyone on the list had in common besides death. She just had to discover what it was.

When she discovered what that file meant she knew she would discover why Jane Doe's slides had been removed from her desk and why someone was following her. What were they afraid she would uncover? Once she found the answer she would know why Peaceful, Georgia, was no longer so peaceful for her.

Chapter Seven

Sebastian tightened his hands on the steering wheel and blinked into the early morning sun. He might as well have stayed on Leanne's porch keeping vigil; he hadn't slept a wink because he'd been worried about leaving her. He was certain it hadn't been kids playing pranks the night before, just as he knew someone at Shady Rest was keeping them under surveillance. Now, the net seemed to be tightening.

For some unknown reason, Leanne was a source of concern to someone. Was it because of the secret she was keeping from him? Or was William Lucus merely keeping tabs on what he considered to be his property? The idea aggravated him. But it would tie in, since someone had been watching them during the picnic. Whatever it was, Sebastian didn't like it. And he was going to get to the bottom of it.

Sebastian's dislike of William Lucus had intensified when Lucus had assumed he could arrange Arthur's interment without input from the family. Sebastian pulled to a stop in front of Leanne's bungalow and glanced at his watch. The memorial service wasn't scheduled for another two hours. She probably wouldn't appreciate his early arrival but at this point that seemed trivial. He needed to reassure himself she was all right.

He pushed the doorbell once and waited, loosening his tie slightly. The heat was already oppressive. Today would be another scorcher. The door opened and the temperature suddenly had nothing to do with the warm stirrings in his chest. He had his wish: Leanne's pale golden hair waved down to her shoulders gloriously framing her wide blue eyes, soft full lips and gently rounded chin.

"Sebastian, I wasn't expecting you!" she gasped, pulling her cotton robe more tightly across what was unmistakably bare skin.

Clearing his throat, he attempted a friendly smile. "May I come in? We need to talk."

Without hesitation, she stepped back. "Of course. Come in."

The air-conditioning wasn't much relief, but he relaxed at the open look on her face. She had no artificial barriers up right now.

"Have you had breakfast? Would you like coffee?"

"Coffee with cream, if you have it."

Nodding, she hurried into the kitchen and a moment later returned, handing him a steaming mug.

"Why don't I finish dressing and then we can talk." It wasn't a question, she was already across the room, nearly into the hall.

"Leanne!" His voice halted her.

"Yes?" she asked over her shoulder.

"I like your hair that way."

From across the room, he caught the blush that flooded her cheeks. Without responding, she escaped into her bedroom. Sipping the coffee, he prowled around the living room. He was too restless to sit. Her bookcase was a revelation. Besides the medical volumes, there were also art books, collections of old and new poetry, and the complete works of J. R. R. Tolkien. Placed here and there on the shelves were pictures; one was obviously a graduating class, another had Leanne and Carla flanking William Lucus.

On her desk was a more recent picture of Leanne and William. He picked it up to study it more carefully. His stomach knotted. The expressions on their faces told the complete story. Leanne's smiling face was innocent and trusting. She was totally at ease within the haven of William's arm, but his face held a fine edge of possession. Perhaps only another man would have the perception to recognize it.

"What have you got there?"

He turned and saw her standing in the doorway. A soft blue dress that exactly matched her eyes revealed alluring curves, just as her robe had. He blinked and forced himself to behave. It wouldn't do to alienate her now. Instead of the compliment he wished to deliver, he said, "I was just admiring this photo of you and William. You both look happy."

"Thank you, it was taken just after I came here. He was my advisor at med school. I would have never got through if it wasn't for William. I'm happy to be able to work near him again."

He replaced the picture, careful not to reveal his feelings. He knew that what was really going on had never entered her mind. She didn't know William wanted her. They weren't lovers! That gave Sebastian pleasure, even if it was out of proportion to what he should probably be feeling, given the circumstances.

"William is quite a guy," Sebastian drawled, turning back to her, not missing her raised eyebrows. "Sorry. I've recognized he's almost sacrosanct in these parts, but I'm not exactly thrilled that he had my uncle cremated before I even arrived. If he had held off the way he should have, I would have been able to say goodbye properly. And perhaps some of the other family members could have been here for the services."

Her chin jutted into the air. "I'm sure William had a very good reason for doing whatever he did."

"So he says." Immediately Sebastian realized that his blatant dislike of William wouldn't bring Leanne any closer to trusting him and he backed off. "Leanne, I know you're hiding something or protecting someone. We haven't known each other very long and you have no reason to trust me. But I have to know one thing. Does my uncle's death have anything to do with whatever it is?"

That heart-stopping vulnerability broke across her face. She stared earnestly up at him. "You deserve an honest answer. All I can say is, I just don't know."

Something primal erupted to life; he clenched his fists at his side. "If there was any foul play involved in Uncle Arthur's death, I don't care who you're protecting, I'll get to the bottom of it!"

She stared pointedly at his fists and, slowly, he released them, the rage spent as quickly as it had come.

"Sorry." Running his fingers through his hair, he paced away from her. "It's just my frustration coming through. None of this makes any sense. I guess part of it is that I haven't quite accepted Arthur's death. Even though I hadn't seen him for a while, he had been such a big part of my life that when I found him, I thought we'd have more time together.''

He gripped and ungripped his hands, not caring that he was betraying his emotions. ''He looked so well when I saw him—just a vague complaint about his hip. To have him gone so suddenly, to not be able to say goodbye...''

''That's what today is for,'' she interrupted, trying to offer some consolation. ''A time for us all to say goodbye.''

He went on as if he hadn't even heard her. ''And then to get back here and find everything taken out of my hands. All the arrangements were made and Arthur's will hardly made sense.'' He walked over and stood directly in Leanne's path.

''He left everything he had—money, books, and all his research—to some foundation, The Amaranthine Society. I've never heard of it. It must have something to do with astronomy, though. That was his ruling passion. I know he'd want to help the research continue.'' He shook his head. ''Something just doesn't seem right. And, if there is something wrong, I want to take action, not wait around for the next shoe to fall.'' He paused. ''Sorry to make you the brunt of all my frustrations and anger.''

Nervously, she tightened the hair she'd carefully coiled at her nape; a frown marred her beautiful mouth. ''That name seems familiar. Perhaps Arthur mentioned it once.'' Shrugging, she shook her head. ''I wish I could tell you more, but I can't. If I had any real information for you, any proof, I'd tell you. But I've nothing, only suspicions. Until I know more, I'm not going to risk telling anything."

She moved around the room, gathering her keys, purse and a handful of tissues. She stopped and said pointedly, "I must stop by the hospital and see a few patients before the memorial service."

She was trying to don her cool, detached persona but he knew her well enough now that he could see right through it. And he very much liked what he saw. "Fine! I'm going with you. I'll wait and then we'll go to the Pickerell Chapel together."

She shot him a startled look from her wide, blue eyes; her mouth quivered in what was not quite a smile. "I don't need a watchdog, Sebastian."

"I'm not sure about that. I'm ready whenever you are."

To his surprise, after a cool appraisal, she picked up her briefcase. He followed her out the door, more determined than ever to discover the secrets she was hiding from him.

She spent the rest of the morning under Sebastian's eye. Literally. She felt the energy his very presence generated and he was being a watchdog, but both traits combined for her benefit were enough to topple even the most determined of individuals.

He was charming, helpful, and supportive as she performed her duties at the hospital. So much so that guilt weighed heavily on her conscience. She'd already admitted to herself that she would trust him if the current situation concerned only her. But what *really* did she have to tell him?

All she knew was that someone had taken slides from her desk and then replaced them. Dr. Anthony Montague had lied to her concerning why he wouldn't discuss Marcus. She had, through what amounted to nothing less than snooping, found a list of names that was curious, considering half of the people were long deceased. Finally, someone was following her. That was it. But what made it all so curious was that these things had begun with her questioning of Jane Doe's perfect preservation. All she'd done since then was take one day at a time, trying to unravel clues. Her own gut instinct insisted something was wrong.

Sebastian was silent as they drove to the service. The closer they got to the chapel the more jumbled her thoughts became. But when they entered the hushed atmosphere, it was quite simple to focus on the reason she was there. Arthur Kincaid had touched many lives. The old, mahogany pews were full. Flowers banked the altar and extended down the side aisles. The combined scents of roses, lilies, and carnations hung like a fragrant cloud over the room.

Sebastian led her to the empty front pew reserved for the family. "Amazing Grace" was being sung by a local choir. Leanne could feel Sebastian grow tense beside her, but was unsure of how to help him. At the end of the hymn, William approached the pulpit. He was in his milieu. The commanding presence, the mane of pure white hair and the compelling voice riveted every eye to him. His eulogy was stirring, amusing and heartrending. He spoke of Arthur's contributions to science, his wonderfully warm charm and humor, and his abiding affection for his friends in Peaceful who were here to say farewell.

Sensing Sebastian's increasing distress, Leanne finally reached out and covered his hand, which rested on his knee. When he clasped her fingers tightly, capturing them, she didn't resist. Strangely happy that she could offer him this support, she relaxed beside him.

The choir sang "Rock of Ages," then Clarence Pickerell stood to recite the facts of Arthur's life. Clarence went about his duty as he had many times before. His voice was deep and soothing and Leanne wondered how she could have ever mistrusted him. As the final music played, there wasn't a dry eye, including her own, in the chapel. She noticed that through it all William seemed to be staring right at her and Sebastian. Perhaps he was trying to guess the depth of their grief. When William and Clarence stepped down from the pulpit area, people began to stir and slowly file out.

Leanne's hand was still held in Sebastian's tight clasp, and she was content to stay seated until he was ready to leave. William stopped at their pew and appeared to be ready to offer condolences, but she silenced him with a shake of her head. She felt his thoughtful gaze linger on their entwined hands and knew William understood. He left her and Sebastian alone and went outside.

Finally, when the chapel was empty, she leaned toward Sebastian and whispered, "Are you all right?"

"I will be," he replied hoarsely. Then he turned his head, staring at her, his eyes compelling in their darkness. "As Uncle Arthur would have said, you're a darling." Raising her hand to his lips, he pressed a kiss on her palm. "Thank you for being here with me."

Today was a day for sad farewells, Leanne thought. It was not the time to crack inside and let all the pent-up emotions she'd kept under lock and key for years flood out. She couldn't let herself go, not now, in the midst of the fears that haunted her dreams and her days. But there didn't seem any way to stop the flow of feeling that drew her toward Sebastian.

"Mr. Kincaid, I'm sorry to disturb you, but I need to speak to you, please." Clarence Pickerell's voice broke through the pounding in her ears.

Grateful for the reprieve, she gently pulled her hand away and stood. Sebastian's eyes grew even darker. He sent her a lingering glance before he straightened his shoulders and turned to the funeral director.

"Yes, Mr. Pickerell. What can I do for you?"

The placid smile included her. "If Dr. Hunt will excuse us, there is some business we need to conduct in my office."

"Go ahead, Sebastian. I'll wait outside for you."

His mouth curled at the corners; his eyes still studied her. "Don't go away. I'll be right back."

She watched both men disappear through the back door, then slowly wandered through the empty chapel, touching a rose petal here and there. Arthur was gone, but he'd live forever in her memory. She exited onto a wide veranda. Clusters of people stood talking, as if they were waiting for something. William separated himself from Mary, Dr. Montague and Carla. He quickly crossed to where Leanne stood in the shade.

"How is Sebastian doing?"

Remembering the beauty of his eulogy, she reached out her hand. He took it, holding her fingers much as

Sebastian had done. "Your eulogy was wonderful. I know Sebastian was as touched as we all were."

"Arthur was dear to our hearts. He'll be missed. Everyone is coming back to Shady Rest for a light lunch that Mary's organized. We'll reminisce. Would you like to drive with me?"

"I'm going to wait for Sebastian." Gently pulling her hand free, she smiled. "You all go ahead. We'll be along as soon as he finishes his business with Clarence."

"Don't be too long."

It wasn't a command because it was accompanied by his spellbinding smile, but there had been an odd edge in William's voice. Leanne blamed it on emotion. After all, he'd just lost an old, dear friend. She leaned against a cool, stone pillar and watched the mourners drive away. The yard was empty now. The early afternoon sun was so intense she had to move farther back into the shadows to fully escape its power.

Since she was out of sight, she was free to watch Sebastian's progress down the walkway between the chapel and the home itself. Was it just the sun's glare bleaching his skin white, or had something happened? Then she saw that he held a small, black urn in front of him. It brought her rushing forward to meet him. "That isn't—?" She couldn't even complete the question.

"Yes, it is. Mr. Pickerell says it's customary for family members to place the ashes in the glass-enclosed niche at the columbarium."

Bewilderment wasn't something she'd ever seen on Sebastian's face before. He took a deep, ragged breath and looked up at her. His eyes suddenly cleared.

"I think we should get on with it. Would you mind driving my car while I hold this? I don't know the way to the mausoleum."

Leanne drove the few miles so slowly it took almost twice as long to get there as usual. All the time, she kept glancing over to where Sebastian held the metal urn firmly on his lap. It had a top, and was in all probability sealed. But it was nerve-racking nonetheless. She had seen innumerable corpses and attended any number of funerals, but the idea that all Arthur had been was fit into this container made her singularly uneasy.

Sebastian seemed to have shaken off his initial shock. He strode purposefully into the mausoleum, carrying the urn more naturally now. During her year in Peaceful, she'd never had the occasion to be in the columbarium section before. She stopped, gazing at its serene beauty. Large stained glass windows threw prisms of color on the cool, white marble floor. In a corner fountain, water cascaded over an artistic arrangement of copper leaves and fell into a pool where small goldfish swam. A large copper chandelier hung from the ceiling, its lights dimmed discreetly. Watercolor paintings adorned the walls between the glass-enclosed niches. Each niche was marked with a brass nameplate.

One small glass door was open midway down the room. Arthur S. Kincaid was already engraved on the brass plate below it, with the dates of his birth and death. Black wrought iron benches were placed here and there. Sebastian's dark eyes were lost in thought. Sebastian placed the urn in the glass niche, then he slid onto the bench closest to his uncle's final resting place.

Leanne stepped away, giving him these moments of privacy. Actually, the columbarium was very soothing, conducive to quiet contemplation, with the play of colored lights on the floor and the background music of the cascading water.

She wandered along the far wall lost in thought. Suddenly she stopped. Florence Chambers's name was engraved on a plaque right at her fingertips. She searched the wall. Sure enough, two niches over and one down was Lois Martin's name. Her heart banged painfully against her ribs. She backtracked, slowly searching the nameplates. Lawrence Haverstrom's name practically leaped at her. She drew in too sharply on a breath. She felt so light-headed that she reached out her hand and leaned for a minute against the cool wall. Could they all be here?

Blinking rapidly, she pushed herself away, her eyes scanning the remaining section. She crossed the marble floor to another wall. They were all here; the names on the death list. Marcus's made another she realized, her pulse racing. If all the people on the first list had been cremated, where did he fit in?

Was cremation his choice when the time came? Was that the common thread? Was there something different about these cremations that was tied to Dr. Montague's mysterious research? How could she find out? Arthur! Spinning around she saw Sebastian reach up to seal the urn in its spot with glass.

"No, wait!"

Her shout echoed against all the stone surfaces, mingling with the rapid click of her heels.

"Leanne, what is it? Here, sit down. You're as pale as a ghost." He nearly pushed her onto the bench. "Do you feel ill again?"

"No! Listen, Sebastian, I want you to do something for me." Without realizing it, she was clasping the sleeve of his jacket. "I want you to take your uncle's ashes to NASA or Washington or somewhere and have them analyzed."

He didn't tell her she was crazy or sick. He didn't demand answers; he simply studied her with his wide, compelling eyes.

"What are we looking for, Leanne?" he finally asked quietly.

"I don't know. I only know there is something very wrong here. When you get the results it might become clear to me and I'll tell you everything I suspect." She released her grip on his jacket sleeve.

"You've got a deal!" Twining their fingers together, he pulled her to her feet. "But you're going to the Cape with me."

"No, I can't!" She tried to pull away and she shook her head, even though a part of her wanted to keep this tight grip on his hand and go with him to safety. "I have my duties at the hospital. We're already short staffed."

His face set, he crossed to the niche and pulled the urn out. Then he pushed the glass door shut. He grabbed her hand again, refusing to release it. They walked outside and across the parking lot.

"I can't go with you! Sebastian, did you hear what I said?" she demanded. He practically stuffed her into the car and shut her door.

He slid in on his side and nodded. "Yes, I hear you. I don't like it, but I understand." His mouth tightened and he practically glared at her. "I'm taking you home and I expect you to stay safely there except when you're at the hospital. Go straight there and back. Don't take any chances." He thrust the urn at her. "Here, hold this."

She held it tightly on her lap, her fingers growing numb on the black metal. Was she doing the right thing? Now that she had some minutes to think, she began second-guessing herself. Then she realized Sebastian never second-guessed her. He trusted her judgment without really knowing anything. If he could do that, then surely she could trust her instincts, too.

He stopped the car in front of her bungalow. His fingers gripped the back of her neck, below her heavy coil of hair. He forced her to face him. "I'm not coming in because the sooner I get those ashes analyzed, the sooner you'll level with me. But I want a promise, Leanne. You'll sit tight on whatever you've got until I get back."

Reacting to his intensity, she nodded. She was rewarded with a softening of his dark eyes. Suddenly, the fingers at her nape urged her toward him. Lowering his head, his mouth met hers and clung. For one desperate instant she responded, her lips soft and pliable beneath his. Then the kiss was over, but his eyes still blazed at her.

"Get into that house and lock the door. I'll call you tonight from the Cape."

Mutely, she handed him the urn. He buckled it into the seat belt, to keep the contents as steady as possible.

"I'm not leaving 'til you're safe in the house."

She sped up the steps, unlocked the front door with trembling fingers, then watched from the living room window as he roared off.

"I'm sorry, Sebastian. But I can't wait for the other shoe to drop either." She whispered her apology as his car disappeared around the corner.

She had no choice, she kept telling herself on the way to Shady Rest. She had to get another look at that file, to see what had happened to Arthur's name. Had it been crossed off one list and added to the other? If there was a clue she'd missed, she would find it now. And she'd be sure to memorize the name of the file this time. After that, she had every intention of telling William, so he could extricate himself before she told Sebastian.

She left her car at the end of the long drive, out of sight, and walked the rest of the way, trying to keep in the shade of the magnolia trees. Her dress clung to her in the heat, but a sudden slight breeze came up, cooling her. She glanced up. Large black clouds gathered from the east. She couldn't remember the last time she'd watched a weather forecast. It appeared that a new front was coming in. At last there'd be a break in the unbearable humidity, she thought.

The gathering storm wasn't putting a damper on the poolside luncheon. Leanne heard voices and the splash of water. She kept out of sight, constantly alert as she let herself into the administration building. This was the perfect opportunity. All the mourners were involved elsewhere, so she'd try to get into Dr. Montague's office again.

The infirmary door that led to the stairs was locked. But this time, she had her purse. Taking out a credit card, she slid it up and down, jiggled it and tried to jimmy the lock. Did this stuff only work on television? If it didn't do the job, she swore she'd get a screwdriver and take the damn door off its hinges!

There was no sound, only a piercing sharp sensation along her spine. She instantly recognized it. She whirled around, adrenaline surging through her veins.

"Well, well, Dr. Hunt! What excuse are you going to use this time?" Dr. Montague asked quite cordially. His thin lips twisted in a half smile as he stood, blocking the only escape.

Chapter Eight

Hiding the card in a fist, she straightened her shoulders and stared at him calmly. Her heart was beating so hard she nearly trembled with its force.

"Dr. Montague, I was just knocking at this door trying to find you. We haven't had a chance to discuss Arthur's case. I don't even know the official cause of death as written on the certificate. As his principal physician, I should have that information for my files."

He didn't blink an eye. "Heart failure, Dr. Hunt. Arthur passed away peacefully while napping."

He clicked the infirmary door shut behind him and took two steps toward her. "Now, do you want to tell me why you're trying to break into the basement with a credit card?"

The sense of menace that she'd felt in her dream froze her in place now. He approached slowly; his thin lips pressed into a tight line on his narrow face.

Desperately she protested, "I wasn't *breaking* in! I'm an unofficial member of the staff here and have the run of the place, in case you weren't aware of it!" She hoped she exhibited cool indignation.

"I'm very aware of exactly what your status here is, Dr. Hunt. I, however, am not so indulgent as my colleagues. I won't allow my research to be disrupted by your constant meddling!"

He was so close now she could plainly see the red anger throbbing on his neck and face. Suddenly infuriated, she decided she would not be so intimidated. She stepped to the nurses' station and reached for the phone.

"Why don't I call William at the pool area so you can put your concerns to him? I haven't interrupted your research in any way. In fact, I haven't even seen your lab. Just exactly what is it you're doing here, Doctor?" she challenged.

Picking up the receiver, she dialed. His narrowed eyes watched her, and a chill ran down her spine at his confident smile.

"Mary, this is Leanne." She paused, trying to quiet the quiver in her voice. "I'm in the infirmary. Would you please send William here?"

"Yes." He nodded, with an odd twist to his mouth. "Perhaps it is time to bring *everything* out in the open."

The threat of William's appearance didn't disturb Dr. Montague in the slightest and that lack of concern admittedly shook her. If he was up to something, the last thing he'd want would be for Leanne to share her concerns with William.

She had hardly put the phone down when the door burst open. It was obvious from William's ruddy face and ragged breathing that he had run all the way from the pool. For a man of his age, in this heat, it was a dangerous thing to do. The thought that she might have innocently endangered him frightened her and sent her rushing to his side.

"William, sit down!"

He shook his head; his broad shoulders were stubbornly erect. "Leanne, I'm fine. But what's going on here? Mary said you sounded frantic." He shot a sharp look from beneath his lowered white brows at Anthony Montague. "Is there a problem?"

Before Montague could reply, Leanne jumped in, determined to end this once and for all. Then William would be safe. She could be honest with Sebastian; that was something she very much wanted to do.

"Yes, there is a problem! Dr. Montague has accused me of trying to break into his office. He's right. I think it's time we all talked about what's going on around here."

Stunned silence followed her pronouncement. Leanne sustained William's penetrating gaze, a challenge that had sent fear pounding through the hearts of more than one aspiring doctor.

"Let's go to my office. Now!" This time there was no mistaking the command in William's powerful voice.

Leanne agreed with him, glad to get away from the infirmary and that damn infuriating door that blocked the way to the answers she needed. She was beginning to second-guess her decision to come here. After all, she had promised Sebastian she would wait for his return!

William settled behind his antique desk, once more under control, his breathing steady and his color back to normal. Anthony Montague chose a leather chair in a corner behind her. Instead of sitting and allowing him to be out of her sight, she elected to stand where she could see them both plainly.

William motioned her to another chair. "Sit down, Leanne. Let's just all calm down while we clear up this misunderstanding."

His voice was soothing and eminently reasonable. In contrast, she sounded like a petulant child. "No, I prefer to stand. I want to tell you what's been going on. It might seem a bit disjointed, but will you hear me out, regardless of how crazy it sounds?"

His eyes widened in shock. "Of course, Leanne. I have utter faith in you, you know that."

William had a knack for saying the right words. Relief flooded through her and she relaxed slightly. Perhaps she could have this all settled by the time Sebastian returned. Regardless, the die was cast, and although Anthony Montague made her acutely uncomfortable, William was here. Together, they would defeat his menace, whatever it was.

"It stared with Jane Doe." Confidently she began to spell out her concerns. "I felt compelled to join Carla in her lab, hoping that at last we could get a positive ID. But the amazing state of her body, the perfect preservation after so many weeks, bewildered me. On a hunch, I had Carla make me some sample slides for study."

William nodded, as if her action were perfectly understandable. At least he was paying careful attention, not like Dr. Montague who sprawled in his chair, appearing totally bored.

"That's when the trouble started," she continued. "I had to go on rounds and put the slides away in my desk. When I got back to my office, they were gone.

William, you know me. I did not misplace those slides. I remember perfectly well where they were supposed to be. They just weren't there!'' She stole a glance at Montague but he returned her look blandly, as if the events had nothing to do with him.

''The next day the slides were back in my desk, but in a different drawer.''

''Did you examine them then, Leanne?'' William asked quietly, his gaze never leaving her face.

''Yes. And that's what's so weird. They appeared to be perfectly normal.''

''So, what's the problem? Why does the fact that you misplaced some slides bring you snooping around my research?'' Dr. Montague asked.

''Let Leanne finish, Anthony,'' William commanded, although his voice was soft. Nodding to her, he smiled gently. ''Go on.''

Taking a deep breath, she ignored the outburst. She was encouraged by William's understanding. ''Then Marcus Jacobs checked himself out of the hospital without warning. I knew he was under a strain and his test results were bad, but there had never been an indication he wouldn't continue treatment. I went to his house to persuade him to come back. His wife told me he had already gone to seek alternative treatment. Then she refused to tell me anything about it because the *doctor* had warned her not to divulge anything.'' She threw a pointed look at Anthony Montague but he seemed perfectly relaxed in his chair.

''I'm sure that Anthony—''

But Dr. Montague did not seem willing to say anything. Leanne continued, ''Joyce was terrified. She'd inadvertently let Dr. Montague's name slip out. When

I confronted him, he lied to me, saying that the family had asked for confidentiality. That blatant lie on top of Joyce's obvious terror made me suspect his activities here.''

It gave her some satisfaction that Dr. Montague didn't try to defend himself. He actually sat up straighter and looked at William. So did she.

He appeared to gravely consider the matter. ''Is there anything else?''

Although embarrassed, she met his gaze openly. ''Because of my concern, I did something I'm not proud of. I went through Dr. Montague's desk down in the basement. There was a folder that contained two lists of names. The people on the first list are all dead, except for Marcus Jacobs, whose name is penciled in at the bottom. But, William, the second sheet contained the names of you and me and all our friends. And strangely enough, Marcus's name was marked out on that list. It all seems so implausible, I know, but I'm afraid the doctor is using you and Shady Rest for his own questionable activities.''

She saw sadness fill William's eyes before he even spoke. ''Anthony, I believe you should address Leanne's concerns.''

The odd twist in Anthony Montague's mouth sent quivers down her spine. Why did he look like a cat with a canary?

''Dr. Hunt, I have no idea about your slides. But about Joyce Jacobs, I can only say I regret her deep distress over her husband's condition, which obviously accounts for her confusion. I hear that Marcus is coming along well with the new therapy, but the eventual outcome, of course, is still unknown.'' His apologetic look was laced with a mockery he couldn't quite conceal and it sent hot anger tingling through her veins.

"Now, about the file. As you know, I've recently moved. When shifting things around, some folders were inevitably misplaced. I've been looking for just that one. I'm not sure how those two pages got stuck together but I certainly can explain them. The first sheet is indeed of deceased patients who have been part of my study. Marcus's name doesn't really belong there. I must have been talking to Joyce and just wrote his name down." He shrugged, smiling. "I often doodle while on the phone. The second list is of local professionals we are planning to invite to the official opening of our laboratory facility. I crossed Marcus off because he wouldn't be available."

His smooth explanation, the ready answers for all her questions, did not bring the relief they should have. Oh, they were good answers, even plausible, but they didn't explain everything.

"If there is nothing wrong here, why am I being followed?"

"Followed!" William erupted out of the chair, his face flushed with emotion. "What are you talking about, Leanne?"

"When Sebastian took me home last night an intruder was lurking around my house. Sebastian chased him, but he got away. Sebastian said he'd felt someone watching me. And I felt it, too."

"That settles it, Leanne. You're to move out here immediately and for good. Have you called Sheriff Sullivan?"

Lifting her chin, she could be nothing but honest with him. "I didn't call the sheriff because I thought it might be somehow connected to what I believed were Dr. Montague's suspicious activities. I didn't want you implicated by association."

For the first time in their relationship, she could see she had truly surprised him. With a slight movement of his magnificent head, he sent Anthony from the room.

"Leanne." He breathed her name and came around the desk to take her hands. "I don't need protecting. All these admittedly upsetting occurrences aren't connected in any way. The lists you saw are exactly what Anthony says they are."

"William, as much as I admire Lewis, he wouldn't be on an invitation list of local professionals."

Her words only deepened the concern in his eyes.

"Lewis is on the list because he will be handling the audiovisual equipment for the presentation."

She was nearly numb with confusion. His palms slid over her arms and up her shoulders, taking her into a friendly hug.

"I'm sorry you've been so worried. You've been working much too hard for much too long. To my knowledge, you've never taken a vacation. But you must now, for your own health." He squeezed her protectively. "I'll arrange for your leave of absence from the hospital and we'll go away for a few weeks together. You're always telling me I work too hard for a man of my years." He punctuated his last words with a soft smile that revealed the extent of their deep friendship.

"William, why won't you tell me about Dr. Montague's study? Why is everyone so secretive about it?" The words came hoarsely from her burning throat. She wanted so much to believe in him, but she'd been suspicious too long to just let it go.

He shook his head and tightly gripped her hands, numbing her fingers. "Leanne, I want to share it with you. It is something that will revolutionize medicine. And, as such, it's extremely controversial. That accounts for the secrecy. While we're away, perhaps we can discuss it. I know you'll share my enthusiasm."

His absolute certainty was a great comfort. Smiling into his eyes, she gently extricated her hands. "You make it sound very tempting. Let me sleep on it, all right?"

Nodding, he stepped back and guilt pierced her heart as she saw his vain attempt to hide his disappointment.

"I'll come by in the morning, Leanne. Everything will make perfect sense tomorrow once you've really thought it through."

Old habits were impossible to break. At the half open door, she swung around to face him. "William, you taught me to follow my own instincts in everything, medicine included. My instincts tell me something isn't right. Sebastian went to the Cape, to analyze Arthur's ashes. I don't know why, but I feel I'll have some real answers when he returns. Until then, I just don't know what to believe."

She didn't wait for a response, but spun out of the room. In the reception area, before they could pretend they hadn't heard her parting words, she confronted an astonished Anthony Montague, a patently disbelieving Carla, and a stricken Mary.

She swept past them without speaking and ran down the stairs. It might all be a jumble of disconnected incidents, but the common thread was her instinct. For some reason, she couldn't let go of it, particularly since Sebastian shared her feelings. Surely that must mean she wasn't simply letting her imagination run riot.

The wind whipped strands of hair loose; they blew across her face as she ran to her car. Billowing black clouds covered the sun, bringing an odd colored twilight to the late afternoon. She'd never seen the sky look quite so menacing. Lewis's truck looked more green than blue; it idled beside her parked car. He got out of the truck.

"Hey, there you are, Dr. Hunt. Got car troubles? Want me to take a look?"

He sounded like his normal self, which made Leanne laugh in breathless relief. "No, thanks, Lewis. The car's fine. I just decided to walk up to the administration building."

Opening the door for her, he shook his head. "You ought to be more careful, Dr. Hunt. There's a real bad storm coming." He shut her door.

She watched through the windshield while he climbed into his truck and roared away. Only then did she make a careful U-turn and drive back to Peaceful.

She'd thought confronting Dr. Montague and William would bring everything to a head and alleviate all her fears and uncertainties. Instead, they had been intensified. Dr. Montague's explanations made perfect sense, but why would a miscellaneous file be under lock and key? And he couldn't explain the missing slides or the fact that someone was watching her. It frightened her that, at some level deep inside her, she had turned her back on William and was rushing home to wait for Sebastian's call. She kept checking her rearview mirror. Was she being paranoid?

She didn't feel safe until she was home with the doors securely locked. She flipped on the TV and was amazed to hear the coast was bracing for a major hurricane. How long had she been out of touch with the real world?

She checked her emergency supplies. She had enough food and water, no matter what happened. She was afraid to use the phone, so she didn't even check in with the hospital. Finally she settled down to wait for Sebastian's call in her bathrobe; the weather channel still played faintly in the background.

The path of the storm was going to miss the Cape she noted with relief. But suddenly it struck her that Sebastian wouldn't be able to make it back. Alarmed, she jumped up to check her locks. Was she so eager to see him again because he represented safety? Or because he stirred feelings she'd kept tightly locked away?

She was so on edge that she actually reached for the phone when the doorbell rang. Pulling her bathrobe tighter, she parted the curtains to see who was on the porch.

"Mary!" Surprise made her fumble a little with the lock before yanking the door open. "Mary, what are you doing here so late? It's almost dark and you hate driving at night."

Mary's arms were weighted down with an enormous picnic basket. She shook her head, bustling past Leanne. "Well, I followed you as quickly as I could. Someone has to take care of you. It's obvious you're overwrought!" Sighing, she lowered the basket to the coffee table and lifted out a wrapped plate of brownies, another of small sandwiches, a selection of fruit, and a large glass jug of what looked like iced tea.

"I brought you some leftovers from the luncheon." Placing her hands on her hips, she gazed accusingly at Leanne. "I'll bet you've had nothing to eat all day, have you, dear?"

"No, and I'm starving!" To prove it, Leanne dived into the plate of brownies. "These are your recipe, aren't they? They're the best!"

"Thank you, dear. Here, try a cookie while I get us ice and glasses for the tea."

Leanne knew there was no stopping Mary, so she sank into the couch and let Mary wait on her. Grateful for this chance to apologize, Leanne accepted the glass of tea and smiled. Mary settled in beside her.

"Mary, thank you. This was so kind. I'm sorry about today, I—"

"No need for apology, dear," Mary interrupted, patting Leanne's arm as she often did. "It's obvious you're overly tired. I remember you saying you weren't sleeping well. I know how difficult that can be. It can get you quite disoriented. It's all right for us old folks, but not for one of our finest doctors." Taking one small sip of tea, she placed her glass on the table. "Now I'm going to run and let you rest before it gets too dark. Do get some sleep, Leanne dear. As William said, everything will look better in the morning.''

So they had all overheard her conversation with William. Musing on that, she hardly noticed when Mary departed nearly as quickly as she'd come. Munching on a brownie, Leanne watched the car pull away. Her stomach rumbling in appreciation, Leanne consumed some fruit, a sandwich, and a large glass of tea. She wrapped the rest of the food and stored it in the kitchen. By the time she finished, she was yawning.

She wandered into the bedroom and glanced at the clock. She flung herself across the bedspread. She'd just wait here until Sebastian called. She wouldn't tell him what she'd done until he arrived. It was best to confess that she'd broken a promise when they were face-to-face, she decided, stifling another yawn. Slipping a pillow from beneath the spread, she settled her cheek into its softness. Her eyelids fluttered open and she gazed at the clock. She'd actually dozed off for a few minutes. Shaking her head, she widened her eyes, trying to stay awake. She was a light sleeper. She'd trained herself to sleep lightly for when she was on call, so there was no way the ringing phone wouldn't wake her.

It must have. She wasn't consciously aware of the rings, but suddenly she realized that the phone was at her ear.

''Leanne, is that you?''

Despite the heavy static she could just make out Sebastian's voice.

''Yes, it's me.'' She yawned, but even through her sleepiness a jolt of anticipation curled through her.

She was so tired that she couldn't remember what she'd wanted to say to him. It didn't matter. It was so good to hear his voice, what little of it she could. "Sebastian, I can hardly hear you."

"Leanne, what did you say? I can hardly hear you." His voice crackled, fading in and out, adding to the fuzziness of her thoughts.

"Call me in the morning, Sebastian. I'm fine," she promised. She sighed, already half asleep again.

"What's that? Call in the morning?" She could tell he was shouting, but he sounded weak and very far away.

"Good night." She could barely hear his response. She dropped the receiver back into its cradle. His call added to her complete feeling of calm as she settled deeper into the pillow. She must really need sleep. Why else would her body crave it with such urgency?

"I'M SORRY FOR THE STATIC, sir. We're still getting a recording at that number."

"Thank you, operator." Swearing under his breath, Sebastian hung up and resumed his pacing. It had been the same story all night. He'd tried to call her back a number of times. All were totally unsatisfactory. Now, this morning, he still couldn't get through at all. High winds must have taken some lines down during the night. He should have obeyed his initial instinct and not left her there alone, he chided himself. He picked up the phone again, but this time he asked for Peaceful Community Hospital.

Long minutes passed while he grew more restless.

"Peaceful Community Hospital. How may I help you?"

Well at least he'd gotten through to them.

"Dr. Leanne Hunt, please."

"I'm sorry, the doctor is not in the hospital. You can leave a message—"

The line went dead suddenly. He swore loudly and violently. Suddenly the years fell away and Sebastian was again trying to phone Jessica at her lab. He'd been too late. The whole building had been reduced to rubble because she'd broken her promise to stop working on the experiment all her colleagues had warned was too risky. Was this déjà vu? Had Leanne broken her promise not to put herself in more danger? The agony of not knowing twisted his gut. There was only one thing to do.

Charlie Abers, NASA security chief, looked as surprised to see him at this early hour as he had the night before when Sebastian had demanded to have Arthur's ashes analyzed by Charlie's carbon dating team. He'd also requested all the data on The Amaranthine Society to which Arthur had left his assets. Sebastian was trying to cover every angle he could think of.

"Sebastian, what are you doing back so soon? I told you I couldn't get your info until later today," Charlie groused with his usual toothy grin.

"I know, but I can't wait. I want to hitch a ride up to Peaceful, Georgia. Someone must be heading north this morning."

"Cheez, not demanding are we?" Lifting his brows, Charlie swung around and picked up the phone.

Pacing to the watercooler, Sebastian downed three full cups of cold water. Charlie hung up the phone.

"Well?"

"Bosworth says if you get to the airstrip in ten minutes you can hitch a ride with him to Jacksonville. He'll take you by chopper to Peaceful, but says he's dumping you quick and getting out before the storm hits. The hurricane is moving inland and he wants to get up to his folks. You'd better get a move on. And remember you owe me, buddy!"

The last was yelled at Sebastian's back as he ran down the hill. He couldn't quite shake the feeling about Jessica and Leanne being in similar situations. His newly recognized feelings for Leanne shook him to the core. He made it to the airstrip in five minutes and was climbing into the chopper in under ten.

"Hey, Kincaid, I've got Charlie on the radio!" Bosworth yelled. The propellers sputtered, warming up for takeoff.

Adjusting the earphones, he heard Charlie's voice. "Sebastian, you there?"

"Yeah, I read you, Charlie. What's up?"

"Got those results for you. Never say I'm not good, buddy." Charlie's laugh made Bosworth twist around and flick Sebastian a smile.

"So tell me," Sebastian ordered, so tense he was nearly holding his breath.

"The Amaranthine Society is some kind of medical research foundation. But it's so well organized with dummy boards, we haven't discovered what their focus is yet. We're still checking for you. And the carbon boys say the ashes *are* homo sapiens, but dated eighty years ago. That's it, buddy. Have a good flight. Over and out."

Sebastian sat motionless for a full minute, hardly aware the chopper was lifting from the ground. One thought pierced through his shock. Leanne *was* on to something. And someone had been watching, maybe waiting, to stop her.

"Bosworth!" he barked into the mouthpiece. "I don't care what it takes, get me to Peaceful as soon as possible!"

LEANNE STRETCHED, slowly opening her eyes. Her robe was twisted around her, the knot of the belt digging into her stomach. She'd slept all night on top of the spread. Boy, she must have been tired!

Yawning, she sat up, glancing at the bedside clock. She had some time before rounds, before William would be here demanding an answer. How could she give it without knowing what Sebastian had uncovered? She could barely remember Sebastian's call, but she smiled, experiencing again that stirring of emotion.

Automatically she picked up the phone and dialed information. There was so much static she could hardly hear the operator. "Information for Cape Canaveral, Florida, please." She nearly shouted to be heard.

"No...Madam...Hurricane...id..."

Straining to hear, Leanne closed her eyes, concentrating. "Trouble on the line, operator?"

Making out a faint "yes," she hung up the phone.

The crackling had intensified the fuzziness in her mind, but one thing seemed to be coming through clearly. For some reason, she was confident that if Sebastian had anything important to tell her he'd get through. That dynamic energy of his wouldn't let a mere storm stop him.

Trying to shake her lingering fatigue, she took a tepid shower, ending with a cold rinse. Waking up to the beating icy water, she felt revived enough for a quick jog. That should banish the last stubborn cobwebs. Besides, maybe a jog would help clear her mind. How should she proceed in the face of William's logic versus her gut feelings? It was so new, and a little scary, to be at odds with William.

Amazed at how cool the air felt, she glanced up at the sky. It looked as if the storm was near. She turned left from her house, heading toward the outskirts of town, just for a two-mile run. That way she wouldn't get soaked when those clouds finally let loose. She hit her stride along the main road. There was very little traffic and even less when she took the loop road that would lead her back in another mile.

She always tensed a little and slowed when she saw oncoming traffic. She very carefully edged farther away on the shoulder. But when she heard sounds of a car approaching from the rear, she maintained her stride, feeling secure on the other side of the road.

Only when the car seemed to be racing right on top of her did she glance around. In that split second, she jumped out of the way, but pain exploded through her, collapsing her knees and wrenching her stomach muscles upward. She heard herself scream and heard the roar of the engine, but she was detached from it. From high above she watched her body roll onto the asphalt. She'd avoided the car, but her head struck the road. Her body continued to roll until it stopped against the guardrail. A streak of blue mingled with blackness until she saw nothing.

Chapter Nine

Sebastian saw the little town laid out neatly below him. There was the squat hospital and a few blocks away Leanne's neat bungalow. Damn it! Where could they land?

"There! The football field!" Bosworth yelled above the whirl of the chopper blade.

Sebastian nodded, bracing himself. With the helicopter hovering only a foot above the ground, he tossed his duffel bag and jumped after it. Hunched over, he waited as the chopper immediately lifted, swinging up and over the stadium seats. They were just ahead of the storm front and the wind was starting to pick up. Bosworth would have a bumpy ride up to Folkston, but he'd make it.

The stadium gate was locked with a chain so Sebastian had to scale the fence. He heaved his bag over then climbed up and dropped to the ground on the other side. He looked around, getting his bearings. To his right he could see the smokestack of the hospital. Leanne's house would be closer. He'd stop there first just in case she was home, he decided as he took off at a run.

The house looked empty. He sprinted up the steps to the porch. Taking a long gasping breath he beat on the front door and jabbed at the bell. When she didn't answer, he tried to force the lock but it held, so he ran around to the back door and tried again. At least the locks were secure.

She'd promised to sit tight, to not put herself in danger. She must be at the hospital working. That thought pounded through his mind with a force that matched the pace of his heart. He raced for the hospital entrance.

SHE OPENED HER EYES, staring up into the distorted faces of Carla, Mary, Lewis, and William. She wondered where she was and how much time had passed. She realized she was in the middle of her dream. Wait! William's face shouldn't be distorted. It hadn't been the last time she'd had this dream, nor had there been someone insistently calling her name.

"Leanne! Leanne, focus on me! Leanne! Damn it, Leanne, can you hear me?"

Carla's angry voice penetrated through her fog. She blinked, clearing her vision and everything came into focus. All her friends were standing around her. She was laid out on a gurney. The glare of the lights above them made her head throb.

"How did I get here?" Was that really her voice sounding so weak and raspy?

There were murmurs of relief and William's voice whispered, "Thank goodness."

"You've had an accident, Leanne," Carla continued to shout. The sound reverberated through Leanne's throbbing temples.

"There's no need to yell, Carla. I can hear you."

She was glad to hear that her voice sounded stronger already. Struggling to her elbows, she looked down her body and at the white bandage wrapped tightly from her toes to her knee.

"Anything else besides the sprained ankle?"

"A possible concussion," William answered, motioning Carla aside. He urged Leanne to lie back down. "Severe bruising at the hip. That's all, Leanne. Believe me, we've run every other test to make sure you don't have more extensive injuries. All you need now is rest. And regardless of what you say, I'm taking you away to make sure you get it."

His commanding tone brought a smile to Mary's pale face. She patted Leanne's hand. "Yes, Leanne. Don't worry, we're going to make sure you get all the rest you need."

Crystallizing in Leanne's throbbing head were scenes of Mary pouring her glasses of iced tea, feeding her, and afterwards her giving in to overwhelming, incredible fatigue. Why hadn't she recognized her unnatural sleepiness for what it was?

She pulled her hand away, looking from one to the other of her friends, suddenly unsure. Her gaze shifted to Lewis. He stood off to the side as usual, but he was always around. Lewis and his blue truck. Revelation struck with deathly fear. There had been a flash of blue just before everything went black. Had Lewis tried to kill her?

"Here, Leanne. I'm going to give you something for pain." Carla lifted a syringe, purging the air through the tip of the needle. It was a simple motion Leanne had seen countless times. Suddenly, she bolted upright, pushing against William's constraining hand.

"No! Stay away from me, all of you!"

The instant the words burst from her parched lips she regretted them. She clasped trembling hands over her mouth when she saw them react with hurt or shock. Lewis retreated a step and Mary began sobbing.

Carla glared at her. "Leanne, get a grip on yourself!" she said, trying to grab Leanne's flailing arm.

William stopped Carla with a gentle hand. "Leanne, will you let me give you the shot?"

There was such love, concern and compassion in William's eyes that a sob caught at the back of Leanne's throat. What was wrong with her? Why was she afraid?

"Leanne!" Sebastian's voice shattered the tension into a million pieces. Breaking through some barrier deep inside her, it released all her pent-up emotion.

The sobs no longer hung at the back of her throat; they burst out. "Sebastian! You're here!"

His arms gathered her to his chest. His hand smoothed her hair down her back and brought such comfort that she wept against his neck, the taste of him and salty tears mingling against her lips.

"It's all right . . . it's all right. I'm here now," he whispered into her ear, rocking her ever so gently until she quieted. "I've been looking everywhere for you."

The accelerated beat of her heart slowed, but not to its natural rhythm. She was clinging to Sebastian so tightly she couldn't tell whose heartbeat she felt, his or her own. Eventually, with real regret, she slowly placed her palms flat against his chest and separated them so she could look into his eyes. They were dark and wide. Glints of some powerful emotion formed pinpoints of light in their depths.

He lifted her chin with strong fingers. "What happened, Leanne?"

"She was a victim of a hit and run. She's exhibiting obvious signs of shock," Carla replied coolly. "She has to be admitted tonight so we can monitor her possible concussion."

Leanne's palms clenched, gathering parts of his shirt in her fingers. "I don't want to stay here."

"Then why don't you come to Shady Rest? We have all the equipment in the infirmary to monitor you tonight."

Leanne wasn't immune to the pain that she heard in William's voice and saw marked on his face, but her gaze slid back to Sebastian. "I want to go home."

Just as before, he didn't ask any questions. He simply nodded, the cleft in his chin deepening. "All right, Leanne. I'll take you home."

"Someone has to wake her every three hours. I assume you're volunteering for that duty, Mr. Kincaid?" Carla's mocking smile wasn't lost on any of them.

Sebastian's only response was to lift Leanne off the gurney and against his chest. "I haven't got a car. Does this hospital have an ambulance?"

"I'll drive you. Let me get my car and I'll meet you at the front entrance." Without waiting for a reply, William stalked away from them.

Burying her face against Sebastian's throat, Leanne closed her eyes. She didn't want to deal with Carla's sarcastic warning to remember the signs of more severe cranial damage.

"I'm not sure Leanne isn't already exhibiting symptoms." Mary staggered to a chair and collapsed, still sobbing.

Lewis took another look around and then disappeared quietly. There was only Sebastian left. For the moment she felt safe. He shifted her effortlessly and strode down the hall.

"I thought I asked you to stay put," he muttered.

"I'm sorry you have to carry me." She didn't want to argue with him right now.

"You're a lightweight. A little darling, remember?" he whispered, before pressing a kiss on her forehead.

Coils of heat tightened around her chest and she laughed softly, trying to release them. "I'm hardly little. Five-eight in my stocking feet. I'm an amazon!"

"It's all in your head. But if *little* bothers you, I'll just call you my darling. There's William."

Before she could fully digest what he'd said, he was easing her into the back seat of William's car. He climbed in the front and they rode in silence the short distance to her house.

When William pulled to a stop, Sebastian turned to look at her. "Leanne, where is the key so William can unlock your door? I'll carry you in."

"Under the hibiscus planter on the front porch. I don't carry it when I jog."

The minute her words were out his eyes hardened. He got out of the car, moved into the back seat, and then swept her up. "What the hell were you doing out jogging when you were supposed to stay put?'' he bit out. His voice was vastly different than when it had uttered his earlier sweet whispers.

She was saved from answering by William's broad silhouette, which loomed in the open door. The living room light glowed behind him. Sebastian pushed past William and eased her carefully down on the couch.

''If you don't mind, Sebastian, I'd like to speak to Leanne alone. Perhaps you could fix her a cup of tea. She prefers the Earl Grey tea with one teaspoon of sugar.''

Sebastian's face hardened, masking his soft dimple. He looked fierce. Ready to take on the world for her. He looked wonderful.

''Tea would be nice.'' She flashed Sebastian a defensive smile. Would he understand without her putting it into words?

Her coils of tension relaxed. He nodded, spinning on his heels to disappear into the kitchen. She stared after him, realizing they seemed to be communicating on a new level, where only glances and gestures were needed.

William stood over her for an instant before he folded down beside her, taking one hand between his palms. ''I know you better than anyone, Leanne. It isn't shock making you behave this way, it's fear. Fear of us, your friends. Do you know what that does to me? Do you know how I felt when I found you in the roadway?''

The anguish crumbled the strong bones of his face and brought hot stinging tears to her eyes. This man had been the center of her adoration, her respect, her trust, and even her love, the little she allowed herself to express, for years. She couldn't bear to hurt him in any way.

"William, it's not you! It could never be you. You must know that!" The ache of tears behind her eyes made her head throb painfully, but she wouldn't give in to it. She had to make him understand. "I was afraid because I suddenly realized Mary has been drugging me."

"Mary!" He crushed her fingers in his grip, his face so incredulous that there was no doubting his shock. "Leanne, how is that possible?"

Licking a tear from her upper lip, she shook her head. "The last few times Mary has given me food or iced tea I've fallen instantly asleep. It happened at Shady Rest the night Arthur died. Last night, she did the same thing. Why would she do it, William?" Her voice caught on the last words.

Seeing her anguish, William raised her hand to his lips. "I don't know. But I will get to the bottom of this, I promise you," he pledged in the voice that she'd always believed. "You know I'd never let anything hurt you."

How long had Sebastian stood there with a tray, staring at them? The power of that stare brought William slowly to his feet.

"Take good care of her, Sebastian."

"You can count on it," he said tersely.

Something dangerous flashed between them, its force jolting through her like a bolt of lightning.

With careful dignity, William reached down and brushed her shoulder with his hand. "I'll see you tomorrow, Leanne. Rest well."

He'd never looked more magnificent than when he moved away, shutting the door firmly behind him. Nor had she ever seen such brittle anger in Sebastian's eyes.

"I just realized you and William don't like one another. Why? You hardly know him."

The flare of powerful emotion lighted his eyes nearly to amber and his gaze locked with hers.

"Probably because we both want to be your lover."

Had the throbbing pain in her head made her misunderstand the words? "Excuse me? I don't think I understand you, Sebastian."

He placed the tea tray on the table and sat down beside her. "I'm sorry. Let's forget it. This isn't the time to discuss my feelings about William."

She reached for his arm, unwilling to let the subject drop. The jolt of electricity she'd felt earlier intensified and sent currents of shock sizzling along her nerves.

"If I can believe my ears, you said you both want to be my lover. That's not something I'm prepared to forget."

"Leanne, it's obvious to everyone that William feels deeply about you, perhaps more deeply than you've ever guessed." The dimple was back in his chin. He raised his hand, smoothing her hair off her face. "And I don't just call everyone a lit—my darling. You're not so hard to like, you know, Dr. Hunt."

He leaned toward her, not pressuring her but inviting. Still in the grip of feelings that had burst forth in the hospital, she moved toward him, ever so slightly, but it was enough.

He slid his fingers to her neck and she allowed him to tilt her face upward, only closing her eyes when their lips met. His mouth was cool. He dragged it back and forth, slowly letting her lips warm his. Softening and expanding with aching tension, her lips parted in eager anticipation. All the emotions she'd kept locked away inside and all her fear poured out as they clung together. Her hands tangled in his hair.

Crushing her to him, Sebastian drew a ragged breath against her neck. "It scared the hell out of me when I couldn't get through to you! I practically broke the sound barrier getting here!"

She rested contentedly against him, shocked at the overpowering feelings surging through her. After a moment of silence, she pushed away to study his face, now so serious. He only let her retreat so far, and kept his fingers at her nape, gently massaging.

"I knew you'd get through if you had anything important—" The expression on his face altered suddenly. What was she doing, giving in to these feelings? They had far more important things to deal with. "You found something!" Suddenly it hurt to breathe.

"The ashes are eighty years old. They can't possibly be Uncle Arthur's." He shifted so that both his hands gripped her shoulders gently. "Leanne, you have to tell me what you know."

"They all tried to convince me it was my imagination, but I knew it wasn't." She could hear the disbelief in her voice. "All I have is a disjointed series of events that makes no sense."

"Let me be the judge of that," he declared grimly. "Tell me."

Again she laid out everything that had happened, no matter how insignificant. Sebastian's gentle massage of her shoulders and neck eased the tension, and the understanding in his eyes banished her fear.

"So if everyone on that list was cremated like Arthur, and if his ashes aren't his own, then it stands to reason the other ashes may belong to anyone. Which could mean—"

"They're all still alive and part of Dr. Montague's research," she finished for him. "My two patients and Marcus who's disappeared and Arthur and that little boy... they're alive!" Her voice heightened with excitement. "And they're somewhere near...."

He looked at her with narrowed eyes, questioning.

"Because Montague is here. And Joyce. She said she saw Marcus just the other day." Her hand tapped her forehead, causing her to wince. "What's the matter with me? I should have realized he was nearby when I talked to her."

"Can you think of any place he might have them?"

"I don't now. There's nowhere large enough for equipment, if he's using heavy equipment that is—I just thought of something else." She gripped his forearm fiercely. "Clarence Pickerell is involved. If he's not cremating the real people, where is he getting the ashes?"

Sebastian narrowed his eyes. "I don't know. God, when he handed me that urn there wasn't a flicker of emotion on his face!"

"I told William I asked you to have the ashes analyzed and I think Dr. Montague heard me. He knows we're getting closer."

"Then it's time to go to the authorities." He pushed off the couch and crossed to the phone. "I'm calling the sheriff."

"Wait! Sebastian, what about—?"

"William," he finished for her. "I know you want to protect him, Leanne. But I think his own credentials will do that. I don't like him, but even I find it hard to believe he could be involved in anything unethical. The only thing he's guilty of is an error in judgment. He trusted Dr. Montague. William will be fine."

Slumping back on the couch, she closed her eyes, willing Sebastian's words to be true. No matter what he implied she'd never believe there was anything sexual in William's friendship. Long ago, she'd sensed a kinship between them. He'd been the family she'd never really had. And she hoped she'd repaid him in kind. At med school, he'd told his students they should trust him and depend on him for anything. She had believed him; so had Carla. And there was certainly nothing going on between Carla and William.

No matter what, Leanne still believed in William and loved him as a very special friend. She knew he felt the same. That was the love Sebastian had mistaken for something deeper and stronger.

She looked at Sebastian's straight back. His rich brown hair was a bit shaggy at the neck and those currents of electricity sent little shock waves through her. Why, after years of holding her trust and emotion tightly to her, had she given it to this man? Was it because he had his uncle's dark, compelling eyes? Or was it because he had pierced the shell she had built around her? Scientist she might be, but even she knew there were some things that required no answers. They just were.

He turned. His dark eyes were narrowed to slits. He slowly put the phone down. "I can't get through. The lines must be down because of the storm." He went to the window, pushing aside the drapes to peer outside into the gloom.

Struggling to her feet, Leanne swayed for a second, then adjusted her weight so as not to put pressure on her sprained ankle. She hobbled over to join him.

"Leanne, what are you doing?" he barked out. Still, at the same time, he flung his arm around her shoulders, gathering her to his side, her weight leaning against him.

They stood together, his arm supporting her, her head tucked comfortably against him, and watched the storm rage all about them. Through the driving rain, she saw huge trees twisting and bending in the wind. A garbage can clattered down the street, banging into a parked car.

"This is really something. I've never been in a hurricane before."

"It's the effects of Hurricane David and you haven't seen anything yet. When a storm like this moves overland, there are strong winds and heavy rain for hours. That's what we're getting now. Then the eye passes and the rain stops and the air becomes calm and it's unbelievable. The temperature rises and you can't imagine that such a storm ever existed. But beware, for once the eye moves on, the wind and rain return just as fiercely. We'll probably still have rain for a few days after this blows over. As soon as the wind lets up, we'll go in person to find the sheriff." His arm tightened like a vise around her shoulders. "Damn, there's someone sitting in that car across the street!"

"It can't be. Who would be out at a dangerous time like this?" Even before she met his eyes she knew. Someone was there to watch them.

She peered into the darkness, frustrated. "I don't recognize the car. But it's there and I don't know what kind of car Anthony Montague drives or Clarence. I doubt it's Mary's."

"Mary? Why would she be involved in this?" At last she'd surprised even him.

"Because she's been drugging me. She came by with leftover food from the luncheon and afterwards I was so sleepy I couldn't even talk when you called."

"I remember. It kept me pacing the floor all night." His arm tightened again, his cheek nuzzling the top of her head. "God knows who in this town we can trust. No wonder you were so glad to see me. Well, I'm here now. You're not alone in this anymore."

Another breach in that barrier deep inside her gave way, creating a new ache in her throat. Sharing the burden was so new to her, she'd never realized it would feel so good.

He slowly eased his arm away and, only after making sure she could indeed stand on her own, methodically checked the doors and all the windows just as he'd done before.

"This house is as tight as a drum. We're not going anywhere, but no one's getting in."

He glanced out the window one last time before closing the drapes tightly against the storm and all the other dangers the night held. "You'll be lucky if you don't lose some of those trees. Maybe one will land on that car.''

His presence kept the fear at bay. "If we're not so lucky, we can go out the back way when the storm breaks. My car's parked there, anyway.''

"Good thinking.'' He brushed her hair from her forehead and frowned. "You've got a whopper of a bruise here. Does it hurt?''

"Not much, considering. But I do feel a little weak sometimes.''

"Here, let me carry you to your bedroom,'' he demanded, his voice taut with anxiety.

She stopped him, holding both palms against his chest. "You're not carrying me anywhere. I can walk perfectly fine, thank you.''

To prove it, she stepped cautiously away from him. She found that if she took short, jerky steps she could make quite decent progress. Still by the time she reached the side of her bed, she practically fell into it.

"You're stubborn, aren't you?'' He stood over her, a smile playing at the corners of his mouth.

"Sometimes,'' she sighed, pushing herself up on the pillows. "I'll rest here a minute and then get out of these clothes.''

"I don't suppose you'd let me help you?'' The smile widened, deepening his dimple and lighting his eyes.

"No, thank you. But you could make me some more tea and toast. I'm sure what you made earlier is cold by now and I'm famished.''

"Okay, I can take a hint. I'll knock three times and whistle low before coming in.''

His cheerfulness seemed out of place here. They were trapped in a hurricane with someone watching them, and on the verge of a mystery whose implications shook her very world. Was he putting up a cheerful front for her benefit? If so, he was doing an excellent job.

Elbowing to a sitting position, she shifted her injured leg and stood. Favoring her good ankle, she hobbled to the bathroom and did the best she could to clean up. Instead of wearing her nightgown and robe, she struggled into soft blue sweatpants and a matching sweatshirt. It seemed too intimate to be in bed wearing lingerie with Sebastian here. But she did leave her hair down, waving over her shoulders.

Less than a minute after she crawled onto the bed, true to his word, he knocked three times and whistled, slightly off tune.

"Who goes there?" She laughed.

"Joe sent me." He tangoed into the room, humming the appropriate melody. His eyes slid over her sweat suit, the corners of his mouth twitching. He didn't miss much. But she did get some gratification from the light in his eyes as he gazed at her hair.

"Well, at least we're making progress."

She tilted her chin in defense. "I always wear it down when I'm in bed."

"As I said, progress," he quipped, setting the tray on the nightstand and dropping down beside her.

She stared up at him in amazement. "How can you be so flip! We're in the middle of a hurricane, we're being watched because we have knowledge someone wants to stop us from using, your uncle may be part of some mysterious research project and—"

"Leanne, stop!" To give emphasis to his words he placed his palm gently over her mouth. "I know we're in the middle of a storm and I know we're being watched, but we're safe in here from both. We can't go anywhere but neither can whoever's in the car, and they're in a hell of a lot more danger out there. Yes, we have knowledge and no one can take that away from us. And we're going to use that knowledge to find out what happened to my uncle and the others. All the feelings I have about this are here inside, but right now we can't do anything. Right now, my job is to watch you and make sure you're all right. When it's time to act I will. I have every intention of finding out what's going on."

Blinking rapidly, she touched the curve of his hand and instantly it dropped away. "I understand. And I appreciate all you're doing for me. Even though I know we're in a great deal of danger, I feel safe in here with you."

"Good." He lifted the tray and placed it across her lap. "Here's a banana. My mom always gave them to me when I was sick. I put cinnamon and sugar on your toast." He shrugged. "I like it that way. Eat and then take a nap. This storm isn't going to let up for hours. If I don't wake you every three hours it probably will."

It did. Its power raged around the bungalow, rattling panes, whistling through cracks, slapping its rain against glass. One incredible gale shook the house so much that the bed shuddered beneath her. She sat up in alarm, but Sebastian appeared instantly in the open door.

"Go back to sleep, it's all right."

She snuggled under the afghan he'd thrown over her and closed her eyes. Just as quickly she opened them again, curious. What was he doing?

With a great deal of clumsiness she struggled off the bed and limped into the living room. The couch bore evidence that he'd rested there, but right now he was at the window peering out into the night.

"Are they still there?" she called over the howl of the wind.

Startled, he jerked around and then sighed. "Yeah. But they've moved a few times. There are branches falling all over the road. We've almost got our wish. There's a chance the storm will cause whoever that is real danger."

"Yes, in this wind it's still possible. You said it yourself, they can't do anything to us in the storm. You might as well be comfortable and get some rest. My bed is big enough for both of us." She was glad he didn't try to be humorous, or falsely flirtatious.

He simply nodded. "If you're sure you don't mind."

He followed her slow progress into the bedroom. Although she tried to calm it, her pulse was racing. She lay tensely for the first few minutes after Sebastian settled beside her. Wide awake, convinced she'd never sleep now, she listened to his strong, even breathing until slowly she relaxed and closed her eyes.

An earth-shaking crack and resounding thud that shook the house brought her awake. She was curled into Sebastian's warmth. Tilting her head, she peeked up and found him watching her.

"It's all right. I think we just got our wish. Although I'm sorry about the tree," he whispered, leaning toward her mouth.

She was arching up to meet him when a sharp pain in her side stopped her.

Her moan jerked him to a sudden halt, suspended above her. ''Is it your head?'' he asked quickly, concern darkening his eyes. ''Your ankle?''

''No, my hip,'' she groaned, rolling over onto her back. ''It's bruised from where I tumbled on the road.''

He lay on his side, hovering over her. ''I feel like I'm in that first Indiana Jones movie. Where *doesn't* it hurt, Leanne?''

Delight coiled through her, bringing a sense of fun she didn't even know she possessed. She placed one finger on her lips. ''Here.''

He took the finger, sucked on it gently, then placed his mouth on hers. He nibbled at the corners of her lips and outlined their contours with his tongue until they parted, welcoming him. His taste, his searching, made sensations coil through her. She went willingly when his hands shifted her closer. Her breasts pressed against his chest. That's when she heard bells. Her eyelids flew open and she was captured in his laughing eyes.

''Yes, I heard bells, too. But it's only my watch alarm. It's time to check on our watcher. Don't go away.''

She flung herself back on the pillows. The throbbing of her head, her hip and her ankle had nothing to do with this new awareness inside her.

From the doorway he spoke. ''Leanne, my darling, I'm afraid our fun is over. There's a huge tree trunk across the road and our watcher is gone. Listen . . . the wind has stopped. It's time to go to the sheriff.''

If she hadn't seen it with her own eyes, she wouldn't have believed it. How could he change so quickly from tender to tough? Where all his forceful energy and personality had been focused on her needs before, now it was channeled in a completely different direction.

He made sure her car was running and checked her house. Only when he was positive it was safe did he help her down the back steps. Nearly every street was either blocked by branches or whole trees, or was flooded. At one point, they drove through a yard and just barely managed not to get bogged down in the mud. There was not a single car moving on Main Street when they pulled up in front of the town hall.

The lights were on, but no one was behind the counter. Sebastian rang the bell and then impatiently rang it again.

On the back wall a narrow door opened and the old gentleman from the records room shuffled through. He nodded to her in recognition. "What can I do for you?"

"We need to see Sheriff Sullivan." That restless energy made Sebastian's voice harsh.

The man raised his gray brows under his green visor and shook his head. "Sorry, but he's not here. The bridge is out on the main highway and the river roads are all flooded, so he's out putting up roadblocks. Everyone's got no choice but to stay put. This one's about as bad as Camille back in '69. Better go on home. There's worse coming. Now, I've got to get back to the basement. All my records are on that damp floor."

They stood staring at each other as the man shuffled back the way he had come. Now where could they go? Who could they trust? They were virtually isolated here in Peaceful. There was no phone. No way out of town. No one else to turn to. They only had each other.

Chapter Ten

If they stayed together and stayed calm they could do anything. Leanne was bolstered by Sebastian's absolute confidence. But as much as she wanted to limp home, pull the covers over her head and let Sebastian protect her, she knew she couldn't. She had her own duty to perform.

"Sebastian, I've got to go to the hospital! With all this damage, there must be injuries."

He gripped her shoulders, his eyes hard. "You know we can't get out of town, which would be the smartest thing to do. We're on our own until we find Sheriff Sullivan. You'll have to be on guard every minute, even at the hospital."

"I know, but it's my duty to go."

He flicked a glance up and down her body. "You look like you're the one who needs help. They'll mistake you for a victim."

"The *they* you're talking about is probably only Carla and the nursing staff. They need me and I'm going!"

"Stubborn and beautiful," he muttered, shaking his head. "All right, let's go and see if they really need you."

The noise and chaos in the emergency room was apparent before they even pushed the glass doors open. A man holding a small child knocked them aside, as he flung himself through the door. The waiting room was packed with people. Only one administrative secretary had made it in and she had been pressed into doing light nursing. Janice was sorting cases, making certain the most needy were treated first. Leanne could see that every cubicle in the treatment area was full. Carla was hunched over a gurney setting a broken leg. Next to her Lewis was helping Betty stanch a head wound.

Carla looked up and saw them. "Thank God!" she gasped with real relief, totally devoid of her usual sarcasm. "The guy in two needs stitches."

"Sebastian, shove that stool over here, so I can lean on it!" Leanne ordered. Forgetting her own ankle, she hobbled over and began to take charge. For the next few hours there wasn't time to think of the danger they were in. All she could do was administer to broken bones and lacerations. There were two heart attacks. Whenever she had a chance to glance up, Sebastian was there. He wheeled in patients and IV equipment. He seemed to have a knack for knowing what she needed before she even asked.

Finally, the stream of patients slowed to a trickle, and everything was under control. She sighed deeply and settled onto the stool to nurse her sore ankle. Betty pushed a hamper full of dirty linen out of the way. In the doorway, Sebastian stood talking with Lewis and

Mayor Johnson, who was soaked to the skin and covered with mud to his knees.

As if he felt her gaze, Sebastian turned and quickly crossed to her. He jerked a curtain closed so they were cut off from view.

The expression on his face frightened her. "What is it?" Now that the injured were cared for, she couldn't stop wondering what would happen next.

He took her into his arms, one hand sliding beneath the loose coil of her hastily pinned up hair. His fingers seemed to always find the exact spot where the tension was settled and massage it away gently.

"Mayor Johnson says they need more help sandbagging the river. He says the sheriff is out there and will be for hours. It's our chance to get to him. Are you up to it?"

"Sebastian, I've got to stay here in case we have more patients." She knew it was the right thing to do, but a part of her was frightened to let him out of her sight.

His fingers tightened on her shoulders. "Leanne, we shouldn't be separated. And I have to get to the authorities with what we know."

"Then you should go. Half the town is in this hospital. If anyone threatens me, I'll scream for help. Surely *someone* will listen." She meant to alleviate his fears, but instead her own intensified, suddenly all too real again.

"I've got to go. The river hasn't crested yet and every able-bodied man is needed."

She reached up and touched his cheek. Something in his eyes made her tremble inside. "I'll be okay. Do what you have to do."

The curtain moved and Lewis peeked his head through it. "Sorry, but Mayor Johnson says we've got to get a move on. Are you comin'?"

She saw the decision flicker in Sebastian's eyes; his long mouth firmed in a taut line. "Yes. Give me a minute," he said over his shoulder.

Lewis nodded, letting the curtain fall back in place, secluding them again.

Sebastian's hands urged her closer until her cheek rested against his throat, his arms closing around her. "Promise me you'll stay here, safe. We haven't talked about your accident because I didn't want to frighten you any more. But I think it was a warning."

Wordlessly she nodded, rubbing her cheek against his cotton shirt. She hadn't allowed that idea to really take root in her thoughts, but in her subconscious she'd already recognized the truth.

"Promise me that if anything seems suspicious you'll scream for help. Everyone in this town can't be involved in Montague's scam, damn it!"

"I know. But Mayor Johnson, Lewis and Sheriff Sullivan were on the list." Her palms flat against his chest, she arched back to look into his eyes. "You be careful."

"Hey, don't worry. You were on that list and I trust you...with everything." His mouth curled at the corners, and his eyes searched her features as if memorizing them.

"Are you comin', Mr. Kincaid?" Lewis's voice filtered through the curtain.

Sebastian splayed his fingers over her cheeks, his lips taking hers in a hot urgent kiss that ended much too soon. He pulled away. "I'll be back to get you," he promised, his voice harsh. Then he pushed aside the curtain.

She followed him to the doorway and watched the three men disappear down the hall. For one fleeting instant, it flashed through her mind that this was all a trick. Lewis and Mayor Johnson were spiriting Sebastian away and she'd never see him again. Fear such as she'd never known sent her hobbling out into the hallway.

"Where are you going?"

Carla's voice stopped her. She swung around. "I've got to stop Sebastian."

"Why?" Carla's dark brows lowered in a scowl. "I just saw him leave with Lewis and Mayor Johnson, to sandbag. Your hero again!" She smirked. "Come on back to ER. There's enough to do here. Check that patient in four, while I take a look at two."

Taking a deep breath, Leanne tried to calm her pounding pulse. At least Sebastian wouldn't be alone with Lewis and the mayor. Other men would be there. Sebastian was right, not everyone in Peaceful could be involved. And Sebastian was strong and brave and smart. He'd get back to her no matter what.

A woman who had been cut by flying glass was their last patient. When she was safely sutured and sent home, Leanne sighed. "I'm beat. My ankle hurts and my hip aches. I'm going to my office to rest for a few minutes."

"I'll come with you. We've got to talk about yesterday," Carla declared.

For a fraction of a second Leanne hesitated. Then she dismissed her fears; she'd known Carla since medical school. Even though she was abrasive, she was a talented doctor and she'd never intentionally hurt anyone. She hobbled down the deserted hallways, Carla following silently. Leanne settled into the comfortable desk chair and propped her foot up.

"Sit, Carla," she said gesturing wearily. "I'm sure you're as tired as I am."

Carla refused, placed her palms on the desk, and leaned forward belligerently. "I just want you to know you made a real fool out of yourself yesterday and hurt William. How could you? You've always been his fair-haired girl. And all for nothing. All this nonsense is in your head. I took your stupid slides and I returned them!"

Folding her arms across her chest, Carla glared at Leanne, who sat motionless in shock. "You were making such a fuss about that body that I started to worry. I thought I'd missed something, but I'd already sent all my slides to Tennessee. So I came here looking for you. I found out you were at Shady Rest so I looked in your drawer and there they were. You're usually at William's for hours, so when you popped in my lab I was so shocked and embarrassed at being caught that I didn't say anything. If I'd remembered what damn drawer I got them from you wouldn't be running around town acting like an idiot!"

Dumbfounded, Leanne could only stare up at her. She found her voice. "Thank you for telling me, Carla. I appreciate your honesty."

"Good! Now relax and stop acting like we're all ax murderers!" Spinning on her heels, Carla let the door slam shut behind her.

Leanne rested her head on the chair back and closed her eyes. Suddenly it was all too much to take in. If only Sebastian was here, he could help her sort it all out. The door swung open and she blinked. How could she have fallen asleep and left herself so vulnerable? A man was silhouetted in the hall light.

"Sebastian?" Her voice caught with hope.

"No. It's me. William. I've brought Mary with me."

Leanne gasped, pushing to her feet. It was a Mary Leanne had never seen. Her bustling efficiency was gone. Her shoulders were hunched; her colorless face was marked by red blotches. Her eyes had nearly swollen shut from weeping. Mary stepped toward her.

Involuntarily, Leanne shrank back in her chair.

"Leanne, dear, I never meant to hurt you. I only meant to help you," she sobbed, collapsing in the chair in front of the desk.

Stunned by Mary's obvious remorse, Leanne went around the desk and kneeled in front of her.

"Mary, look at me." She spoke very softly. "Please look at me, Mary."

The ravaged face lifted from the white handkerchief. "I only gave you some of my sleeping pills because you said you weren't sleeping well. And you looked so tired and stressed out. It helps me sleep, so I thought it would help you." Her hand darted out and touched Leanne's arm as it so often did. "Please believe I meant no harm. I just wanted good things for you. After all, you're such a fine doctor, we can't have you getting ill. I was only trying to take care of you."

"I believe you, Mary," Leanne whispered, her own tears burning behind her eyes.

Biting her quivering lip, Mary nodded and stood. "Thank you, Leanne, dear. Thank you for understanding. See, William, you were right. Leanne understands."

William laid one arm across Mary's shoulders and led her to the door. "I know, Mary. I'll be right out. I want to talk to Leanne alone."

Struggling upright, Leanne leaned back on the edge of the desk. She was so shaken by everything that had happened in the last few minutes that she didn't know what to believe. If it wasn't for what Sebastian had uncovered, she could almost lull herself into thinking that this had been some kind of odd string of freakish incidents, with no underlying mystery, just horrendously bad judgment on everyone's part.

"Leanne, can't you see how all of this has gotten blown out of proportion?"

William turned the full force of his personality on her; the commanding presence, the powerful voice, the air of unqualified dignity. She'd seen him do it countless times, bringing student bodies, faculties and scientific communities under his spell.

"What about the people watching me, William?" she asked quietly. She was not quite able to accept all these oh-so-pat explanations.

He took one step closer and shook his head. "Unfortunately, these things happen, even in a small town like this."

"And my accident?" she continued softly, wishing Sebastian was here. How quickly she'd become accustomed to sharing this burden with him!

"Leanne, I'm afraid joggers are injured every day." William stood over her, his eyes clear and bright. "You're overworked and tired. We all understand how you could have misunderstood what you've seen and heard. And of course Mary's ill-conceived plan to help you rest is enough to shake anyone. But everything else has a logical explanation. Now, stop worrying and concentrate on getting well again. You'll see, in a week or so this will all be a foolish memory."

She flung back her head and met his eyes. "Everything? Then explain why Arthur's ashes are eighty years old. They're not Arthur's at all. What's the logical explanation for that?"

The stern set of William's face dissolved for a moment then reassembled in astonished disbelief. "What!"

"Sebastian took the ashes to NASA. They are human, but they were carbon-dated to eighty years ago. They can't possibly be Arthur's ashes."

"There must be some mistake. Maybe Clarence gave Sebastian the wrong urn or—"

"No mistake, William. It's what I've been trying to tell you all along."

"My God, how could this be?" He staggered slightly, then steadied himself with the back of the chair.

"Everyone, including you, has been trying to explain away my fears. Even Carla had a reasonable story to cover the slides disappearing. But do you know what? No one will be able to explain this. And whatever I do, I'm going to find out what happened to Arthur Kincaid."

Coming to rigid attention, he held up his palm. "Now calm down, Leanne. I don't want you to run off somewhere and get hurt again. You've convinced me." His eyes suddenly blazed down at her. "I'll get to the bottom of this! Once and for all!'' He stormed out, letting the door bang against the wall.

She knew she could trust William, but nonetheless she was shaken by her conflicting emotions. She had no choice. She had to learn the truth. She sent a silent, heartfelt apology to Sebastian for breaking yet another promise. She was in luck. William had stopped to talk to Mary at the end of the hall. Leanne turned the other way and went the long way around, pushing her throbbing ankle to its limits.

She was in her car, waiting, when William pulled out of the parking lot. She didn't turn on her lights even though it was raining again. The gray mist made it hard to follow anything. She kept his red taillights just in sight, trying not to be conspicuous.

It was hard to tell in the mist, but surely he should have turned off by now. Her heart gave one uneven stroke when he drove right by the road to the Pickerell and Pickerell Funeral Home. Shouldn't that be his first stop? To confront Clarence about the ashes?

The farther William drove out of town, the more hot fear scalded her throat. She passed the entrance to Shady Rest before she finally guessed where he was going. He turned off on the road south of Shady Rest and she knew he was heading to the mausoleum. There was nothing else down this way but the cemetery.

Switching on her lights, she gunned the motor, taking the shortcut down the Shady Rest lane like a madwoman. Halfway to the villas, she pulled over. She left the car and cut through her jogging trail. The ridge beyond the trees would be a perfect vantage point.

She panted. Her bandage now hung in muddy strips from her leg. She broke through the trees just as the back door of the mausoleum opened. *Damn her ankle*. She hunkered down and peered into the mist. A light went on over the entrance. It was just enough to allow her to see Anthony Montague silhouetted on the threshold. William entered quickly. The door shut and the light went out.

There was some protection from the rain here, but it dribbled down from the overhead branches and mingled with the tears that poured unceasingly down her cheeks. What was Dr. Montague doing at the mausoleum? Could his research center be disguised as the mausoleum? She remembered wondering at its size. Suddenly excited, she crawled forward. Arthur would be there!

Halting, she realized she needed help. William had come to confront Montague alone! She bit her lip, stopping her sobs, waiting to see if William came out. If anything happened to him because of her, she'd never forgive herself.

The wind howled through the trees and she shivered when it sent a shower of fat raindrops down her body. The door remained shut. Below her, on the road, she heard a car. She could see lights progressing through the wall of rain. She hid behind a tree as Lewis's truck pulled to a stop. He walked up to a side door and unlocked it, then returned to his truck. He began hurriedly to unload yellow canisters and carry them inside. Was everyone in town part of this?

Then she remembered Sebastian. If Lewis was here, where was Sebastian?

She tore back through the woods. Branches tangled in her hair, scratching her arms. When she reached the clearing, the wind caught her, whipping strands of hair into her face, blinding her. Its force was so great she had to fight to get the car door open, only to have it ripped out of her hands. Crawling in, she used both arms to finally slam the door shut, cocooning her in the warmth and safety of the car.

Her ankle was beyond pain. There was a stitch in her side and she felt as if she'd been in a prizefight. But she had to find Sebastian! She took great gulping sobs like a child, blinking to see through the windshield. It was awash with sheets of rain. Where was her cool detachment, the wall she'd shielded herself with for years?

It was gone and had left only rubble in its wake. Sebastian had breached her protective walls. If they got out of this nightmare in one piece she wasn't going to ever again be afraid to live her life fully. And that meant not being afraid to trust and love.

For one heart-stopping moment she remembered how she'd felt when he walked out with Lewis and the mayor, that raging fear that she might never see him again. She pressed the accelerator and gripped the wheel with trembling fingers. She'd find him; she didn't care what it took!

THE AIR WAS SO UTTERLY still after the violence of the storm that it was eerie. While they sandbagged against the raging torrent, which only yesterday had been a placid stream, Sebastian saw men continually glancing up, assessing the sky. He'd been working for hours and he still hadn't had a chance to find the sheriff. Still, he couldn't desert his post. The team working this part of the river was really shorthanded.

He didn't want to stay away from Leanne too long!
Hell, this *was* too long. Five minutes was too long, he
raged, taking his frustrations out by doubling his pace.
He shifted sandbags so quickly that the man next to
him couldn't keep up.

A flashing bubble light drew his attention. The
sheriff's car finally stopped about a block up the road.
Stepping out of the human chain that passed the bags
man to man, he fought his way through the oozing
mud to where the sheriff consulted with Mayor Johnson. Suddenly the mayor rushed away, and the sheriff
started to back up. In one lunge Sebastian smacked the
window with his muddy palm.

Instantly the glass rolled down again. "What the
hell are you doing?" Glaring, the sheriff frowned up
at him, then nodded. "I know you. You're Arthur
Kincaid's nephew from the Cape. What are you doing here?"

"I've got to talk to you, Sheriff. It's urgent!"

"Well if it's urgent, climb in. I've got to head back
to town and you can tell me on the way."

Sebastian climbed in. The interior of the car smelled
like cigar smoke. Sebastian flashed an apologetic
smile; he was literally covered with mud and so would
be the seat.

"Don't fuss about this old junker. Looks like hell,
but it gets us where we're going." The sheriff's laugh
came from deep inside his barrel chest. "It'll take us
a while to get back into town with all the detours, so
you might as well start telling me what's on your
mind."

Leanne had implied that the sheriff lacked imagination. There was no point in trying to outline all their

vague feelings and doubts. Sheriff Sullivan didn't believe in intuition. "You know my uncle's memorial service was a few days ago."

"Yep, sorry to hear it. He was a nice old guy." Small eyes set above puffy red cheeks flicked him a cool look. "This problem of yours has got something to do with your uncle dying?"

Tired and worried to distraction about Leanne, Sebastian was in no mood to mince words. "I'm not sure he's dead. I had the ashes Clarence Pickerell gave me as my uncle's remains analyzed by NASA. They aren't his. Their carbon date is eighty years ago. I'm not sure what happened to my uncle, but I am sure Clarence Pickerell and perhaps Dr. Anthony Montague are involved in something unethical and probably illegal."

While Sebastian was talking, the sheriff's ruddy complexion turned nearly purple. "Listen here, Mr. Kincaid. I don't know much about Dr. Montague, but Clarence has lived in this town his whole life." He snorted, anger sharpening his drawl. "He's no criminal! The only crime he's ever committed is not being the businessman his granddaddy and daddy were! Where're these ashes? Got 'em with you?"

"I left them at the Cape." Sebastian kept his anger banked even though he knew what was coming next.

"Not that you fellas at the Cape aren't mighty smart—hell, you got us to the moon—but I've got to have the evidence before I can make any accusations. Besides, Clarence is at a morticians' conference in St. Louis. He won't be back until next week. Got to give him a chance to defend himself."

Sebastian took a long, controlling breath. "What about Dr. Montague?"

"What's he done, anyway?"

What indeed, Sebastian raged. He balled his hands into fists at his sides. "Someone has been prowling around Leanne Hunt's bungalow and someone nearly ran her over with a car yesterday! What do you intend to do about that?" Sebastian spit the words out between taut lips. He was so angry he wasn't sure he could resist smashing something.

"That pretty doctor, heh? Well, now this sounds like a matter for the police. As soon as this crisis is over, I'll look into it." The sheriff's puffy face split into a grin and he shot a sly look at Sebastian. "I've seen you and Dr. Hunt together. I figure you'll be keeping an eye on her, but tell her I said to be extra careful for the next few days."

"I'm sure she'll be reassured by that!" Sebastian's sarcasm went right over the sheriff's head.

"Stop here! I'll walk the block to the hospital. I'm sure you have more important problems to deal with." Sebastian got out of the car and slammed the door without a backward glance. There was only one thing to do. He had to get Leanne out of this town now!

The ER was empty except for Carla who was bandaging an arm wound. "Where's Leanne!" Sebastian demanded loudly. He wasn't surprised when Carla glared at him.

"I haven't seen her for a while. Maybe she went home."

He swiveled, running outside to scan the parking lot. Her car was gone.

She's got to be at home, he told himself over and over again as he sprinted to her house. The car wasn't there and neither was Leanne. Frustrated, he banged on the door with his fist, hoping maybe she was inside after all. Still, there was no answer. He leaned his forehead against the door, taking long, deep breaths, his heart pounding so hard he was shaking with it.

This wasn't like Jessica any longer. Nothing he'd ever experienced matched the raw desperate ache tearing him apart inside. He'd felt guilt when Jessica was killed because there was nothing between them. There hadn't been in years; maybe there never had been. They were both so tied up in their work that their marriage had been little more than a convenience. When job opportunities across the country separated them, it had barely rippled the routine of their lives. Somehow they had just slipped apart.

Helping Leanne had made him reach down inside and search through all that guilt. In doing that, despite his reservations, he'd filled the hollow with something new, with someone else. Kincaid men only fell in love once, and he knew now that it had finally happened to him.

He pushed himself upright, taking a deep breath. If he had to tear this town apart, he would find her. And he was never, ever, letting her out of his sight again! The wind had come up, swirling the rain in front of it. He dashed off the porch and swung around the side of the house. He came face-to-face with Leanne.

Her breath caught in her throat when she saw the look of stunned joy on his face. He caught her in his arms and she tilted her head, meeting his eager mouth with a desperation of her own. The rain beat down and the wind howled around them and still they clung together until a shiver began deep inside her, spreading outward.

Gasping, he pulled away. "We've got to get inside," he shouted over the wind and rain.

They literally fell through the back door, making muddy puddles on the kitchen floor. His hair was plastered down by the rain and he was filthy, but he looked wonderful to her. His hand left a streak of dirt on the door when he double locked it. Anger and relief fought a battle in his eyes. Finally, he touched her nose with a cold finger.

"You look like you're the one who's been sandbagging. Where did you go?"

"Not now, Sebastian. I'm freezing and so are you. We're here and safe for the time being and that's all that counts." They were both soaked to the skin and shuddering. She stumbled toward the bathroom. "We've got to get in the shower and warm up before we both catch pneumonia!"

He was right behind her. She kicked off her ruined shoes and stepped into the shower stall, turning the water on full force. The hot, soothing water beat against her hair and she turned up her face, letting its warmth caress her chilled skin. Sebastian did the same. Brown muddy water streamed off their bodies and pooled at their feet before disappearing down the drain.

Sebastian shed his shirt, throwing it over the glass shower door. The water made rivulets down the muscles of his chest and Leanne's eyes slowly swept up his body. He was watching her.

Gently, his fingers tangled in her wet hair and caressed her neck. "I thought I'd lost you. It scared the hell out of me! Where were you?"

"Following William. He's gone to confront Dr. Montague. I don't know what's happening." Drawn by feelings so new they scared her, she placed her palms on the hot, wet skin of his chest, giving in to her desire to touch him. "What about the sheriff?"

"He doesn't believe me." Sebastian's eyes dropped to her blouse. It was transparent with moisture as was the flimsy bra beneath.

Once his gaze would have embarrassed her, but now it made her flesh tingle.

"I don't know yet how we're going to do it, but tomorrow we're getting out of this town and finding help." His voice was hoarse; his fingers continued to massage her neck. But this time the tension wasn't fading, it was building and spreading through her whole body. How could she be trembling again when hot water was streaming over her skin?

"Did you hear me, Leanne? I'm getting us out of here tomorrow," he repeated. His hands urged her closer, as if to emphasize his determination.

"We're going to have lots of tomorrows, aren't we, Sebastian?" She could hear the wonder in her voice; it made her smooth her palms slowly up over his shoulders. She tangled her fingers in his hair. "But even if we don't have tomorrow, I want this," she whispered, kissing his shoulder, sliding her mouth over his wet skin to where the pulse quickened at the base of his throat. The impending danger that had brought them together, to this moment, now added to her desperate need to open up to life, to this one man, before it was too late.

"Leanne." He breathed her name against her mouth as his lips explored gently, caressing with such aching tenderness that she arched her breasts against him, wanting to spread this feeling everywhere.

His softly exploring hands fed her need; their mouths clung. She was so immersed in the feel of his body that she became wild and free in a way she'd never known. Amazed at her own eagerness, she helped him with her clothes and met every caress of his mouth, his tongue and his fingers with building pleasure.

Gasping with new sensations, she pressed kisses down his chest, licked away drops of water and hooked her fingers into the waistband of his pants. She boldly unfastened them, pushing them down his slim hips. She glided her hands slowly back up his calves and thighs, teasing him. She finally touched and with that caress such warm passion swept over her that she moaned at his hoarse mutters of encouragement.

Holding her hips between his hands, he slowly, carefully lifted her body over him. He held her there for one breathless moment, not moving, letting her feel his warmth and power, letting the ache inside her intensify so it was hard for her to breathe. His dark eyes searched hers.

"Kincaid men only really love once," he whispered brokenly, looking at her with such raw, exposed feelings that the moment would be imprinted on her memory forever.

"I know," she sighed. She wanted him to know what she was feeling, what she wanted for them. The tension urged her to rub her swollen aching breasts against his damp chest and to press her hips into his. There was no place their bodies were not touching, no place that wasn't overflowing with the tenderness she'd craved.

"Sebastian," she gasped, pulling his head down to meet her waiting mouth.

No matter what tomorrow held, she would always have this moment of love.

Chapter Eleven

The rhythmic beat of the rain on the roof and against the window panes woke her. She didn't even open her eyes, but continued to rest her cheek against Sebastian's warm chest. One arm was flung over him and their legs tangled together comfortably, fitting together like pieces of a complex puzzle. There was no longer any place to hide her feelings, not after last night. And there was no need to hide.

Shouldn't she be shocked by her actions? Shouldn't her unbounded response cause some embarrassment? Instead, she felt immense satisfaction from their night of lovemaking that had taken them from the shower to the bed to an exhausted sleep, wrapped together. Now it was tomorrow. She felt the same. Sebastian was all that she wanted, all that she needed, and nothing could ever take these moments away from her. Suddenly her pulse quickened. She remembered what this day might reveal.

"Leanne, what is it?" he asked. His lips touched her ear; his fingers slid beneath her hair to massage her neck, as though he sensed her sudden tension.

"I was just thinking that it's time to go now, isn't it?" Propping her chin on his shoulder, she stared into his eyes. They were only inches away. "You're right, the only sensible thing to do is to get out of town. Particularly when we don't know who to trust. But I hate leaving William like this. He went to confront Dr. Montague because of me. And now we don't even know if William is all right or not."

With his other hand, Sebastian gently smoothed her hair back, his eyes playing across her features. In their depths, she saw something flicker to life.

"I understand your concern, but it doesn't change our need to get out of here. If I thought William was in any real danger I wouldn't just desert him."

"But I told him about the ashes. Doesn't that knowledge put him at risk just as much as us?" she insisted. She was still unwilling to abandon William if he was in danger.

"And I told Sheriff Sullivan. But I'm not sure either one of them really believes us. That's why we have to get out of here and get to someone who will, someone who can help us get to the bottom of whatever is going on here."

His hand moved over her neck slowly; his eyes followed it. The touch warmed her skin. "About you and William..."

She stopped him by pressing a soft kiss to his lips. "There is no William and me, except as dear friends. I—I hoped I'd made my feelings clear last night."

She was stammering and felt embarrassed. She buried her face against his chest. Hadn't he realized what she was trying to tell him last night? She'd never opened up to anyone, exposing her deepest needs, the way she had to Sebastian.

His chest shuddered in a breath of laughter and she turned to one side, still not looking at him.

"I hope I made myself clear last night, too." His fingers brushed up and down her spine, sending shivers of remembered pleasure. "But just in case I didn't, I plan to rectify that tonight. Hopefully somewhere far away from here, somewhere safe where we can take days to make sure everything is perfectly clear to both of us."

She dared to glance up and smile. "That sounds wonderful. But I have to stop by the hospital first to check my patients and notify administration that I'm taking a few days off. Then we can leave. You can have the shower first."

His grin made her nearly forget the danger. Heat rose in her body when she remembered what had happened in that very shower.

"Care to join me?" he inquired softly, his eyes lit with mischief.

She shot him such a look that he rolled out of bed. She watched him pad to the living room and retrieve his duffel bag, pull out his shaving kit and turn toward the bathroom. A shiver of pleasure curled her deeper into the sheets. He had a marvelous body, compact yet muscular with broad shoulders tapering to narrow hips. Recalling how that skin had felt beneath her fingers sent another shiver down her spine. Desperately she sought to cling to these few moments of stolen time before they had to face whatever dangers today would bring.

THE HOSPITAL WAS QUIET. Everyone was on the job; everything was under control. She headed straight to administration and made her request. It was granted without difficulty. Once that would have surprised her, but under the circumstances she didn't care to question.

"What else is left?" Sebastian stayed very close to her and she could tell he was checking the area around them cautiously.

"First, I want to stop in my office and pick up those slides. I still think they're important. Then I have to see my patients."

She couldn't help thinking the slides might be gone, but when she opened the drawer, there they were, exactly where she'd left them.

Sebastian picked up her phone and quickly put it back down. He shook his head. "Still dead."

Two white sheets of paper were folded on her desk. She recognized Carla's handwriting on the outside of one and opened it. The note was blunt and to the point.

"Carla saw my patients before she went home to sleep off her double duty." She flicked him a small smile. "It's her way of trying to make me feel guilty. But it means we can leave immediately."

"Good! With this additional rain I don't know how far we can get, but at least we're taking some kind of action."

She couldn't concentrate on his voice, all her attention was focused on the words in the second note. They blurred in front of her. It was William's handwriting. William was telling her he knew what was going on and he needed to see her at Shady Rest as soon as possible. She looked up, all traces of triviality gone, and silently handed the note to Sebastian.

It took him only a minute to scan it. "Are you sure this is William's handwriting? It could be a fake. Some kind of trap."

"William wouldn't do that."

"But what if it's not William? What if someone is just trying to lure you out there?"

"You think they have a forger working for them, too? I'm almost positive it's William's writing. And it could be a plea for help. I can't just ignore that."

For a split second she thought that was exactly what he wanted to do. His eyes were hard, his mouth a tight line. "Leanne, we're trying to get out of the lion's den. Not walk right into the lion's jaws."

"I can't leave now without seeing William." Tilting her chin up, she considered what she might do if he refused. Instead of any logical argument she just let him see what she truly felt. "I'm afraid. I don't want to put you in any more danger, but I owe him so much I can't just leave when he might need me."

"All right," he relented. "We'll stop by Shady Rest, then try that road to get as far away from here as possible."

The grim set of his mouth and the hardness in his usually warm, brown eyes never altered on the drive to Shady Rest. The constant rain and the overcast sky made the place appear deserted. Leanne could sense Sebastian's tension. She saw it in the bunched muscles of his shoulders and back, and felt it in the strength of his grip when he touched her. They crossed the path toward the administrative building, Sebastian still monitoring their surroundings.

Despite his misgivings, he was going along with her. She'd always handled her problems alone, except those she had shared with William in school. Now to have Sebastian's support and trust allowed her to reach out to him in new and deeper ways. Someday she'd tell him what this meant to her. Without words, they climbed the carpeted steps and walked down the vacant hall to William's office. Mary's desk sat empty and so did William's.

"I don't like this," Sebastian muttered under his breath, the grip on her hand tightening as his eyes searched the room. "Let's get out of here!" He pulled her back the way they'd come.

All the way down the stairs she didn't resist, but in the foyer she stopped. "I know where Dr. Montague's office is. Let's check there first, just to be sure."

Her whisper sounded too loud in the utter silence that was only broken by the distant sound of the beating rain. She looked around guardedly. Everything seemed perfectly normal. Except no one was here. Now she urged him through the empty infirmary, anxious to get to William. The plain wood door beyond station two was closed, but not locked. She pushed it open and beckoned him through.

From the landing she could see light spilling out into the dark hallway from both downstairs doors. "Someone's down here!"

Her heart pounded so loudly she could hear its rhythm in her ears as she moved forward. Sebastian's presence made her feel somehow safe. The door she'd never been able to open before contained a superbly equipped laboratory.

Sebastian glanced in and paused, but Leanne pulled him to the other door. This office was empty, the desk bare.

"No one's here. Come on, I want to take a better look at that lab!" he said.

"Wait! Just let me check..." She opened every drawer, but there was nothing. Even the normal desk contents of the top drawer had been removed. "Oh, no, it's been cleaned out. I wanted to show you the lists. To see if there was a clue I'd missed."

"Don't worry about it now. With those ashes, we have enough to cause Dr. Montague a great deal of trouble. Come on, I want a look at his lab."

Sebastian seemed strangely eager to explore the other room. To Leanne it appeared to be nothing more than the standard lab, except with newer equipment, but Sebastian was intently interested. He let go of her hand, studying the setup of the experiments and sniffing test tubes. He prowled around the room, here and there opening doors to small refrigerators, picking up containers and reading their contents.

Leanne followed him, perplexed by his interest. She recognized Ringer's solution; it was used in every lab she'd ever seen, but that was it.

"Glycerol solution, adenosine triphosphate." It was almost as if he were talking to himself. His voice rose as he picked up more vials. "Dr. Montague or someone has every high-energy phosphate known to science here."

Moving across the room to a cooling cabinet, he opened it, scanning labels. "Serotonin and norepinephrine! They're using all the same chemicals in experiments at the NASA labs."

Hearing something new in his voice, she rushed toward him. Off to the side was yet another door. It stood half open as if inviting her in. Drawing closer, she heard voices. Angry voices. And angrier and louder than the others, she recognized William's. She'd been right, he was in danger!

"Sebastian, I hear William! He's in trouble!" she called over her shoulder. She flung herself through the door before he could stop her.

At the end of a dark, narrow, tunnellike hall, she saw light and the voices echoed even louder. Without waiting for Sebastian, she ran forward.

He caught her, swinging her around to face him just inside the threshold of what appeared to be a storage closet. The light had come from here, but the voices apparently came from somewhere else; the room was empty.

"Leanne, for God's sake, you can't help him! We've got to get out of here now! It's a trap!"

Picking her up bodily he whirled around and headed back the way they'd come. He only took two steps before the door slammed shut and in their momentum they swayed to a crashing halt against it.

"Damn it! I knew it!" Sebastian said, his eyes darting around the room.

She tore away from him to try another door on the opposite wall. It was locked, just as she knew it would be. She'd led him into a trap. Because of her overwhelming desire to help William, she'd got them both caught.

"Oh, Sebastian, I'm sorry."

"Forget it. Let's just figure a way out." He didn't appear angry or disappointed as he assessed the room.

"William would never be a part of this. He'd never willingly hurt me," she offered.

"Now, that I believe. But he might not be in a position to do anything about it." Sebastian's voice and demeanor was devoid of everything but cool determination as he continued to feel the walls, and stare up, studying the ceiling tiles.

As far as she could see, there was nothing in this room to help them. No boxes, shelves, nothing to batter down the doors, nothing but iron clothes hooks placed all in a row high on the wall.

"I've got an idea! I want you to climb up on my shoulders and see if any of those ceiling panels can be loosened."

He leaned over and she scrambled onto his shoulders. With her head tilted back, she reached up. Icy steam hit her full in the face, robbing her of breath. She flinched and Sebastian swayed backward, knocking against the wall.

He pulled her down from his shoulders and held her tightly next to him. The white steam continued falling from a valve in the ceiling. Across the room, another valve opened and a steady issue of tiny beads hit the floor, rolling crazily and into nothingness.

"I knew it! Liquid nitrogen. Is your face all right?" His fingers ran over her skin and she nodded, stopping his restless movement by cupping his palm to her cheek.

"I'm fine. Sebastian, what's going on?"

Already the temperature in the room began to drop. "This is ridiculous!" She was angry now and frightened. "Long before we could freeze we'll run out of oxygen in here. Someone is trying to suffocate us."

"Yes." Calmly, deliberately he reached for her. "Climb up again. It's our only chance to get out of here!"

The icy cloud of steam hovered at the ceiling so already it was hard to breathe. Her fingers tingled with numbness as they felt along the ceiling for any give in the tiles. Coughing, she ducked her head, needing oxygen to clear her fuzzy brain. Through her harsh gulping intake of air she heard Sebastian's voice.

"Are you all right? Anything yet?"

"No!" Shaking her head she went up again into the icy mist. Her heart pounded, trying to do double duty to bring more oxygen and more blood to her starved organs. Was it her imagination or had two tiles in the corner moved ever so slightly under her probing? The strength in her arms gave out. She moaned in frustration.

Instantly he slid her to the floor, cradling her in his arms.

"Take shallow breaths, Leanne. Slow and shallow," he urged quietly, his voice tight. "Stay on the floor for a while. There's plenty of oxygen left."

"I—think—" She gulped in sweet air, trying to gesture with her head. "Over there . . . right corner. Tiles moved."

Understanding, he nodded. "Stay here." He hastily pressed a kiss on her forehead before leaping up. He scanned the wall and then ripped off his belt and looped it around the hook nearest the corner. Using it as a hoist he scaled the wall, disappearing into the ever-increasing mist to work away at the tiles.

"I think they're coming loose!" With his face set in hard determination, Sebastian lunged upward in one more powerful thrust and Leanne heard the ceiling give way. "I've got it!"

He slid down beside her for a few moments, catching his breath. Then with gentle hands, he lifted her to her feet. She leaned against him, still too light-headed to have any strength.

"Listen, Leanne." Cupping her cheeks, he tilted her face up, searching it. "I'm going to put you on my shoulders again and I want you to grab hold of the opening and hoist yourself through."

This time she couldn't stop swaying once she was on his shoulders. Desperately, she reached up and felt the edge of the opening, but her hands were too tingly to maintain a hold.

Even though he encouraged her, with every attempt it became more futile. "I can't," she admitted at last, sliding down his body. "You go and come back for me."

He wasted one full minute staring into her face.

"Please, Sebastian. It's our only chance." She slumped to her knees and he came with her, kneeling to cradle her in his arms.

"I'll be back. I'll crawl over the ceiling supports to another room with similar tiles, get down and come back for you. Stay low and keep breathing—slow and shallow! I won't take long."

She allowed herself to sway against him for one brief moment and then with weak hands pushed him away. "Go on. Lots of tomorrows, remember?" She giggled from oxygen depletion, and bit her lip trying to stop it.

But she knew he understood. She saw it in his eyes.

"That's my darling! Hold on. I'll be right back!"

By using the belt and bracing against the corner wall he pulled himself as high as he could. Then he braced his foot against the hook and levered up to catch hold of the opening. His body swung free, hanging, before, slowly, he pressed up until his waist was through the ceiling.

"I'm out!" he shouted down. "Stay by the door! I'll be there to get you!"

Crawling to the door, she placed her cheek on the floor where there was more air. Sebastian would come. He'd said so and she believed him.

The door rattled and she pushed to one elbow. He was back already!

The door opened slowly. Through the mist, Leanne saw William. How could that be? They had come to rescue William, but he was perfectly fine. She giggled again and, horrified, bit her lip so hard it sent a jolt of pain along her jaw.

"Leanne! What's going on?" In three steps he had her up off the floor and into his arms. She was too weak to protest that she was too heavy, and that he was too old to hold her like this, particularly in a room nearly devoid of oxygen.

"William—I—"

"Don't try to talk, Leanne. Just breathe," he ordered, striding through corridors that were just a blur to her.

Trying to get her bearings, she looked around. "Where—where are we?"

"I said don't talk! Breathe!" he commanded in his powerful voice. "Don't worry. We're in the mausoleum. There's nothing more to fear. I'm here now."

"Your note—I thought you needed help."

He hesitated, then opened a door into a typical hospital room. She looked around wildly. Where had he brought her? He settled her onto the bed, his face flushed with anger. That told her everything.

"There was no note from you, telling me you know what is going on?" She stared up into his eyes, trying to understand what she saw there.

"Leanne." Taking both her hands between his wide palms, he rubbed them, bringing back feeling. "Leanne, I really do understand now. I've been a terrible fool, but I believe now someone wants to harm you. But I won't allow it! Do you believe me, Leanne?" A ghost of his magnificent smile curved his mouth. "I've never failed you, have I? And I won't now."

"No, you've never failed me. And I know you'd never hurt me."

"Thank you," he whispered, gently pressing a kiss on her forehead. "Rest now. You'll be safe, here." Her hair had fallen loose, waving across her face, and he brushed it back with two gentle fingers. "I'll be back for you. I promise. But stay in this room!"

She closed her eyes and lay back on the bed, feeling a sheet being pulled over her. She willed herself to breathe evenly, normally. The door clicked shut. In a flash she sat up, slightly dizzy but determined. Sebastian would be looking for her. He'd be frantic if she wasn't in that little room. More than ever, she felt danger closing in around her and Sebastian. She had to get back to that closet that had very nearly been their tomb. Sebastian had said he'd come back for her and she knew he would.

William had told her they were in the mausoleum, but when she stood in the doorway all she could see was a hall with no doors. She tried to remember which way they'd come. It seemed as if William had turned right into this room, so she went left now. At the T she could only guess because there was nothing to guide her. She made another left, her stomach knotted in a tight fist of fear. Someone was trying to kill them because they knew too much, of that there was no longer any doubt. Sebastian had been right. This was a trap and she'd led them right into the lion's jaws.

WILD WITH FRUSTRATION and fear for Leanne, Sebastian finally found a loose panel a good six yards beyond where he'd entered this dark and dusty, cramped realm between floors. He pried it up and peered down. The room below was empty. He dropped into it and headed for the door. To make sure he didn't run smack into Anthony Montague or William Lucus or any number of people who were more than likely involved, he stood at the door, listening. When he heard nothing, he cautiously opened it, then ran back down the hall.

The little room stood open and the jets had been turned off. The nitrogen had dissipated quickly, leaving no evidence. Where was she?

He whirled around, searching the long hall, desperation forcing wild plans to go through his head. Desperation was dangerous. To find Leanne he would have to be cautious and methodical. And he would find Leanne no matter what it cost him . . . or anyone else.

214 *The Last Good-night*

THE MAUSOLEUM had never appeared to be so large that it could contain this maze of hallways. Strangely, there were very few doors. Leanne was reluctant to try them in case she ran into Montague. But she feared she'd simply been going in circles; it was beginning to all look the same. Somewhere she had made a wrong turn or surely she would be back to that storage closet.

At the next corner she turned opposite from the way instinct told her to go. Instinct hadn't been working very well. This hall was more dimly lit. The farther she traveled, the darker it got. She trailed a hand along one side of the hall hoping somehow she might stumble on a way out. Finally she stopped and peered up at the ceiling. Here there didn't seem to be square panels, but it was hard to tell in the darkness. Was Sebastian trapped up there looking for a way out?

A fist of fear beat at her stomach, increasing its blows when she heard footsteps coming toward her. Inching along the wall, her hands came in contact with a doorknob. Desperately she turned it and to her amazed relief it moved. She nearly fell into the room. She had barely closed the door before voices and footsteps passed in the hall.

She found herself in a lighted office with a desk littered with papers. But there was a phone. She could call the state police! Someone for help! Eagerly she picked it up, but hope died quickly. There was no dial tone. The lines must still be down. She and Sebastian were on their own, and their world had grown even smaller. They were trapped in this building.

Her eyes fell on one letterhead that was repeated over and over again on papers strewn across the blotter. The Meridan Foundation. Perching on the edge of the chair, she picked up several sheets, studying them. Dr. Montague was head of the Meridan Foundation. According to these invoices, the foundation performed cremations and embalmings. Most of the bills were directed to Pickerell and Pickerell. But the Meridan Foundation was supposed to be doing research on the elderly. She shuffled through the rest of the papers, seeing invoices for thousands of dollars, for some of the chemicals Sebastian had named. She racked her brain, trying to come up with any medical application for the quantities named and failed.

If the Meridan Foundation was doing all of Pickerell's work, then Clarence might be innocent of any foul play. His only crime might be perpetrating the myth he was continuing his grandfather's and father's fine tradition. If the Meridan Foundation was doing all of Pickerell's work, then it was responsible for the condition of Jane Doe's body. And it was responsible for the faulty ashes. But if the Meridan Foundation wasn't really cremating the bodies, what was it doing with them?

There was an oversized file cabinet to her right. Eagerly she rose and pulled open the first drawer. Manila folders were neatly alphabetized. She reached midway into the As. Alkaline. No, that wasn't it! She skipped to Aluminate. Then came Amblygonite.

No file starting *Ama.* Curious, she opened the last one. There were sheets and sheets of reaction formulas, careful notations, meticulously kept. They meant nothing to her; a series of chemical experiments had attempted to put different compounds together. She couldn't begin to guess why.

Disgusted, she slammed the file drawer shut, then swore softly when it made a loud noise. On the other side of the file, a pocket door was set into the wall in such a way that it was difficult to see from the desk or anywhere else in the room. Beneath her fingers it slid open easily. She saw a control panel with dozens of switches and yellow blinking lights, then she saw the surveillance cameras set near the ceiling.

She flattened herself against the wall, inching around the perimeter of the control room, her destination a large, darkened window through which she could see twinkling lights. A door was beside the window on the opposite wall.

If she'd ever trusted her intuition, she did now. All along, as everyone tried to discourage her or explain things away, she had persisted. And that same intuition now screamed at her—beyond that window, in the darkened room, she would find all her answers.

When she was nearly to the first corner, she stopped, listening. A door clicked shut. Someone else was in the office. Her eyes flew toward the sound. She'd left the pocket door ajar!

The fist of fear gripped her insides so tightly she could barely breathe. But she bunched her muscles, ready to bolt as the footsteps came closer and closer. Regardless of her fear she couldn't tear her eyes away from the door. At last she would really know the face of her enemy.

Chapter Twelve

Her heart was in her throat. Joy exploded through her. "Sebastian, stop! There are surveillance cameras up on the wall," she warned him.

He flattened himself against the door on the other side of the control room, his eyes searching the control panel. Suddenly he hunched over and lunged for the panel, pushing a button on the left-hand side. The red lights on the cameras went dark.

A second later Sebastian had her wrapped in his arms, his face buried in her hair. "Are you all right?" His voice was hoarse; he ran his hands urgently over her body. "I was so worried about you! How did you get out?"

"William found me." She breathed deeply, trying to still her racing pulse. Sebastian was here, safe; they were together. "Sebastian, I think this is what we've been looking for."

"I know." Gently releasing her, he stepped to the panel and pushed a button. "We've got to hurry, though. I don't know how long it will take before they realize the cameras are off."

The room on the other side of the window flooded with light. Rows of huge yellow cylinders seemed to go on forever. Something as icy cold as the liquid nitrogen settled in her blood as she walked slowly toward the door. The control room was soundproof she realized. For as she opened the door, she could hear the steady hum of power generators.

Sebastian grabbed her arm. "Let me go first and stay close."

Tentatively, they entered the immense room. Each cylinder sat on a concrete base and was connected overhead to a series of power cables and computer hookups. A few had a light blinking at the top. Those canisters were all near the viewing window. The rest were dark.

Leanne stepped to the second row. On each cylinder in black block letters was printed The Amaranthine Society.

"Amaranthine! That was the word on the file I found!" She placed her trembling hands on her throat and took another step into the chamber.

"It's also the society Arthur left all his money to." Sebastian was so close his breath stirred her hair. "Remember, I told you."

Why hadn't she made the connection? If she had...what difference would it have made? How could she have ever guessed a place like this existed?

"This is a cryotorium, isn't it? There are frozen bodies stored here, aren't there? All those people whose names were in the Amaranthine file..." She felt his hands on her shoulders and was glad for their support.

''But why the secrecy?'' Sebastian's grip tightened. ''Cryonic interment isn't illegal. Just foolish. We've frozen embryos, sperm and some tissue, but no mammal or human organ has ever been revived after being put into cryonic suspension. I know because we're working on it at NASA for deep space exploration. So far, there's no evidence that it can ever be accomplished.''

Her need to see for herself was greater than her shock. She moved away from Sebastian's protective arms and stepped in front of the first cylinder with a blinking light. The glass porthole for viewing was at eye level and she stared into the frozen face of a young boy who hung upside down in a harness. Her insides trembled in revulsion.

Oh, God! At last she understood! Dr. Montague was offering hope where there was none. In the midst of her revulsion came a flicker of understanding. The enemy was death. She knew that. As a doctor, she fought death every day. But Dr. Montague was claiming victory.

He offered hope to the hopeless and the promise of life to the dying. With or without the traditional promise of an afterlife, no one could rationalize the injustice of a young boy dying of leukemia, the injustice of...

''Marcus,'' she whispered. Repressing the nausea burning at the back of her throat, she forced herself to peer into each porthole: there were faces of young and old, men and women, forever still. The terror that she would find what she sought fought with the hope that she wouldn't.

Here in Peaceful the deep fear of death was being banished. Dr. Montague had suddenly appeared, offering immortality through biological technology. And Marcus *had* embraced it. She had seen him look like this in sleep, his high cheekbones made chiseled and lean by his illness, his eyelashes short and sparse above them.

Sebastian peered into the porthole.

"My cancer patient, Marcus Jacobs." She swallowed back hot, aching pain. "I know why all the secrecy." She looked up at Sebastian's pale face. "From what I've read, suspended animation would only be valid if the procedure was started immediately at the time of death. By the time Marcus's tumor would have killed him there would have been nothing left of his brain to preserve. Montague is breaking the law by freezing people while they're still alive."

She saw understanding dawn in his eyes and was grateful she was spared having to say anything more. Now Sebastian peered into portholes. A few at the end of the first row were empty, but in the second row two lights blinked. In one silver tomb they found Arthur Kincaid, his sweet face forever at rest.

Sebastian bent his head, his hands pressed flat against the glass porthole as if he could touch his uncle. Leanne ached because of the pain she saw in his eyes.

Then he jerked away, his jaw rigid. "He killed Uncle Arthur before the Alzheimer's disease completely destroyed his mind. But it doesn't work! The extensive damage caused by freezing alone is enough to kill a human. It can't be repaired. We haven't found the chemicals that will protect the tissues from being destroyed by ice crystals. He deprived my uncle of the last months of his life, for nothing!''

For the first time, his restless intensity frightened her. She'd only seen it used to charm or protect, but she'd never seen it directed against an enemy. Afraid he might do something to endanger himself, she took his arm.

''We won't let him get away with it. We're going to get out of here and stop him once and for all.''

Somehow her quiet voice got through to him. He stared into her eyes. ''You're right. Let's get out of here!''

Hand-in-hand, they ran from the cryotorium, through the control room and to the office door. Sebastian opened it a crack and peered out before venturing into the hall.

''This way,'' he mouthed, turning left. He led her down a maze of short corridors that looked vaguely familiar from her own searching. Then they reached a solid wall and could go no farther.

''Damn it, we took a wrong turn,'' Sebastian mouthed, turning them around.

They took two steps before the sound of approaching voices forced them to open a door and slip inside. While Sebastian listened, Leanne turned to see where they were. It was an observation room for an operating theater. No wonder there were so many halls that seemed to lead nowhere. The huge arena below plus the cryotorium had to be kept virtually inaccessible.

She approached the viewing window at such an angle that anyone glancing up by chance couldn't see her.

She peered down. Three people, who were all dressed in surgical gowns so it was impossible to discern their identities, were performing some kind of surgery. Her stomach lurched! Who were they preying on today?

She had to do something to stop this! She was a doctor. She couldn't allow this to continue. But something was strange down there. Something was missing. Shifting her body, she craned her neck, trying to get a better look.

One of the members of the surgical team moved, exposing the patient's face. Then she knew. For this surgery, the patient didn't require an anesthetic. Even after nine months, Lois Martin's lovely auburn hair streamed away from the pure oval of her face to cascade over the sides of the operating table, as if she were merely sleeping.

This time the shudder in Leanne's stomach sent her trembling back against the wall. She must have made some small sound because Sebastian maneuvered his way to her side.

"What is it, Leanne? What are they doing down there?" He tried to look down, into the operating theater.

"I think they're trying to bring someone back to life."

Tilting her head back she stared into his eyes, willing her voice to be as calm as possible. "I think Dr. Montague believes he's found the chemical combination that will preserve tissue under deep freeze. But like a true madman, he thinks the only way to test his elixir of life is to experiment on humans. The woman on that operating table was a patient of mine who died, or at least I was told she died, nine months ago.''

Tears welled in her eyes. ''That man's a monster! He's been preying on this community in order to get subjects for his research.''

The procedure below them stopped abruptly. The team stripped off their gloves and threw them to the floor. One of the team members stepped forward and draped a sheet over the body while the other two gestured wildly at each other in apparent anger or frustration.

''He was experimenting on my Jane Doe. No wonder my slides disappeared. If I'd been able to study them, I'd have found the ice damage in the cell structure. Sebastian! That means Carla is involved, too. She was covering for Montague.''

His gaze bore into her. ''If Dr. Montague *can* break the ice barrier, he can offer immortality. He becomes the most powerful—''

''He becomes a god,'' Leanne finished, all her fear balled up tightly in her chest. ''But obviously, he hasn't done it yet!''

''No wonder he didn't want you to become too curious!''

She watched the three heads swivel to one particular spot in the room below, a place she couldn't see without revealing herself.

''Sebastian,'' she said softly. ''I think he's just found out we're here. He'll have to stop us.''

''They, Leanne. There are three people in that operating theater. And I'm afraid they're only a fraction of the people involved in Dr. Montague's ghoulish experiment.'' The cleft in his chin dimpled ever so faintly; the hard line of his mouth softened. ''We're going to have to be very creative to get out of here and I think I've got just the thing. Come on!''

Around the corner, a flight of steps led down to the operating theater floor. Without a second thought, Leanne followed him into a scrub room that was off to one side.

''Look for surgical gowns,'' Sebastian whispered.

But the closet was empty; even the disposal barrel was clean.

Sebastian shook his head, his eyes hard. ''Damn it, I—''

Leanne stopped him by putting a finger to her lips. A second later he heard it, too. The operating theater door opened and closed. Somebody was coming toward them. He stepped behind the door and motioned her to crouch behind a linen cart.

The minute the green-clad figure slipped into the room, Sebastian tackled it from behind. He worked skillfully and silently. After one telling blow, the body slumped to the floor. He pulled off the mask. ''Oh, my god, it's a woman,'' Sebastian breathed, his eyes stricken with guilt.

''Betty,'' Leanne gasped. ''Oh, no! Who else is involved in this?'' Then she turned to Sebastian. ''It's not your fault. You had to do it.'' Kneeling beside her, Leanne felt Betty's pulse and lifted her eyelids. ''She'll be fine.''

Leanne felt no guilt, only shock and disbelief. In a million years she would never have suspected Betty's involvement in anything like this. But Montague promised immortality. Perhaps no one was immune to that promise.

Leanne slipped off Betty's surgical cap, picked the mask from the floor where it had fallen, and with Sebastian's help, shifted Betty's body so that her gown could be removed. While Sebastian placed Betty carefully in a locker, Leanne donned the surgical garb.

"Now we wait until someone else comes in to change and grab them, right?"

"Partially right. You get the hell out of here while I wait."

Her heart gave one hard thud against her ribs. Hot tingling sensations made the touch of his hands on her shoulders feel like acid. "No! I'm not leaving you here alone! They want to kill us!"

"That's exactly why you have to go. We both know about this setup. Killing one of us won't solve their problem." He lifted one hand to cup her chin and the touch scorched her skin. "You know it's the right thing to do. Go out through the tunnel and wait for me in the Shady Rest parking lot. If I'm not there in half an hour, leave and head toward Jacksonville. As soon as you see a state trooper, get some help back here."

She tilted her chin, ready to defy the logic of what he was saying. But he refused to let go of her, or to back down. His dark eyes bore into her.

"This is our only chance. I know you want to stay, that this is a battle you want to fight to the end. But going for help is the most important task right now and you're dressed for it! I'll be right behind you as soon as I can, but I want a promise. No matter what happens, no matter what you hear, you keep going. That's the best way to help us both and you know it.''

Leanne had fought and won hard battles in her life, but nothing she'd ever faced was more difficult than this. Logic told her one thing, her heart another, and she was torn to pieces between them.

''Leanne, you've got to go!'' To emphasize his words, he dropped his hands and stepped away. ''Please. For me. For us.''

His quiet plea brought such a rush of pain that she blinked back tears. She would do what he asked but first she had to tell him. ''I think I love you.''

His deep wonderful eyes widened, the cleft in his chin deepened, and he smiled, a glorious smile that blocked out all the danger. ''You *think*. Obviously we need to work on this. Keep that thought until later, okay?''

She tore herself away. The sooner she got out, the sooner she could be back with help.

Sebastian watched her until she was safely in the hall. He didn't want to let her go, but splitting up was the best thing to do for her, for both of them. If one of them got through, the other would be all right. With any luck, he'd be right behind her, anyway. Then he'd spend the rest of his life convincing her that there was no *think* about it. Certainly not for him.

Things were looking up. From his vantage point behind the door, he saw the other two team members come out of the operating theater. They stood in the hall arguing over the procedure for a moment. Then one took a rack of test tubes toward the stairs while the other came toward him.

The figure removed the mask. It was Anthony Montague. Sebastian fought the rush of adrenaline, the urge to strike down the man who had destroyed his uncle. Gauging the right moment, he clasped a hand over Montague's mouth, silencing the doctor's cry for help. Montague jabbed a sharp elbow in Sebastian's stomach, but he hung on, wrestling Montague to the floor. Struggling to keep his grip, he lifted his right fist and landed a sharp clip to Montague's jaw. Shaking out the pain in his hand, he heaved himself to his feet, staring down at the supine body. He hadn't been in a fistfight since he was a teenager.

Leaning over, he ripped off the cap, then flipped Montague over to undo the back of the gown. Pain exploded down his spine, buckling his knees. His last conscious thought was of Leanne.

LEANNE'S SURGICAL MASK covered her face and the cap concealed her hair. She did her best not to run. She wasn't certain of the way, but at least she had figured out that the main corridors encircled the cryotorium. She'd have to branch off to get back to the passageway.

For just a moment she hesitated, then a door opened far to her right. She tried to act natural. She walked confidently toward the man, ignoring the pain in her still tender ankle. It was Betty's husband! Her heart beat so loudly she couldn't believe he didn't hear it. Sebastian had said there were more people involved. But how many? Would the whole town be at the end of that tunnel to stop her!

The storage closet door still stood open. At first she couldn't force herself to go in, then she thought of Sebastian. He was counting on her.

There was one canister on the floor. It hadn't been there before. Someone was using the tunnel. She had no idea who it was or when they'd be back. She'd just have to trust her luck and her disguise.

There was no light at the other end of the dark tunnel, but she knew the main lab was down there. Whatever else might wait for her in that darkness, she had no choice but to go on.

"Don't come any farther, Leanne."

Carla's voice echoed out of the darkness and brought her to a rigid standstill, her mind racing with plans. Maybe, just maybe, she could bluff her way out.

Light glinted off the small gun Carla held in her hand. Gone was Carla's sarcastic smirk. It was replaced by a grim determination.

"Carla, thank God it's you! When did you find out what they're doing here?" Drawing on all her resources, she stared into Carla's face with an air of utmost confidence. "We've got to get out of here and get help!"

"Good try, Leanne! But I'm afraid I can't let you get any more help. You've already caused enough damage."

Leanne took two steps backward, away from the gun Carla shoved into her chest.

"Why couldn't you just keep your nose out of it? Oh, no, Perfect Physician had to get all her answers! You never come to pathology. Why did you have to see that Jane Doe? Your suspicions started then, didn't they?''

''And you had to switch the slides. How long has this been going on?'' Leanne asked.

''We're almost there. We've made incredible progress,'' Carla continued fiercely, her face scarlet. ''Nothing—no one—will stop us.''

''Why, Carla? Why would you get involved in something like this?'' Leanne backed up another step. Relentlessly, Carla was forcing her against the wall. ''It's illegal. It's immoral to kill these people before their full time and then use their bodies like this!''

''Kill them? We're giving them a chance for immortality! He's going to do it, Leanne. Break the ice barrier. And when he does, there will be nothing that isn't laid at our feet.''

Her back pressed to the wall, Leanne stared into Carla's pale face. Carla slowly curled her mouth into the familiar smirk.

''You didn't think we'd let you and your boyfriend stop us, did you? We've known every step you've made.''

''You're the one who's been following me. You ran me off the road.'' If she kept Carla talking, she bought time and Sebastian would come.

''Me, Anthony, Lewis, Betty— Oh, there are so many of us, you just have no idea. But then, you've always been incredibly naive about most things. That's one of the things I've always despised about you.''

Leanne's mind whirled, trying to form some kind of plan, her eyes searching for something to help her. She saw a movement over Carla's shoulder. ''Lewis!''

Her scream startled Carla so much that she turned her head. In that second, Leanne knocked the gun out of her hand. It clattered to the floor, spinning behind the canister. They both dived after it, brushing against Lewis. He stood frozen in the door, holding another canister in his hands. Carla grabbed at Leanne's head trying to stop her, but only came away with the surgical cap.

In one lunge, Leanne had the gun in her hand. She rolled onto her back and pointed it straight up into Carla's red face. "Back off, Carla. Now!"

Carla did as she commanded, backing up next to Lewis.

"Lewis, help me get the gun away from Dr. Hunt. You know she's causing us problems here."

His eyes flicked between her and Carla, then he shook his head. "I don't hold with no killin'. I just do my job to pay for Billy's upkeep and my own when the time comes."

"Lewis, they are killing people here, experimenting. I want you to find some rope and help me tie up Dr. Gregory." Leanne was pleased at how calm her voice sounded even though her insides were trembling. "Then we're going for help."

"Don't be a fool, Lewis!" Carla flashed him a hard look. "She's not going to shoot me or you. But if she manages to stop this experiment, Billy will never have his chance to really live and you will die. You don't want either one of those things to happen, do you? All we have to do is get rid of her once and for all."

She could see the indecision in his eyes. As he slowly lowered the canister to the floor, Leanne's muscles tensed, her fingers tightening around the gun. Her gasp of relief was drowned by Carla's scream of rage.

Lewis grabbed Carla's arms, holding them behind her back. "I told ya I don't hold with no killin'. Got no rope, Dr. Hunt."

His face reddened to match his hair and mustache as Carla thrashed around, trying to get free, all the time cursing him and Leanne.

"Okay. We'll lock her in this room and then go through the tunnel back to Shady Rest. From there we can get help."

"You'll be too late for your lover!" Carla screamed, hate blazing from her eyes.

Fear pulsed through every cell of Leanne's body. "What do you mean?" Stepping closer she stared into Carla's smirking face. "Tell me!"

At her belligerent silence, anger flooded through Leanne, excavating the fear. She placed the gun at Carla's temple. "I've never killed anything in my life, but I swear I'll pull this trigger if you don't tell me what you've done with Sebastian." She hardly recognized her voice as her own, and from Lewis's and Carla's stunned expressions, neither did they.

In a last act of defiance, Carla's mouth curled in a sneer. "We've got him and we're already putting him down for a nice, long nap."

There was no room for fear now, nor was she torn between her heart and her head.

"Lewis, go out through the tunnel and get Sheriff Sullivan or anyone who can help us and get back here fast!"

With Leanne pointing the gun right at her temple, Carla didn't budge when Lewis let go of her. He headed back through the tunnel.

"Wait, Lewis. What is in these containers?" Leanne asked slowly, her gaze locked with Carla's.

"Liquid nitrogen."

Now she smiled, nodding. "Go on, Lewis."

The door slammed shut. She motioned Carla to stand back.

"You're trapped, Leanne," Carla taunted. "No matter what Lewis does, you and your boyfriend will never get out of this alive."

"Then neither will you."

Raising the gun, she pointed it and squeezed the trigger. Carla's scream coincided with the crunch of metal on metal. Liquid nitrogen seeped from the punctured container.

"If I find Sebastian and get back here in time, you should be fine. If not, you suffocate, the way you planned for us to."

Leanne opened the door an instant before Carla reached it. She stepped outside, slammed it before Carla could get through, and then locked it. She listened to Carla's frantic screams and her pounding fists. There wasn't enough liquid nitrogen in that one container to completely deplete the oxygen in the room, but it would give Carla several fearful moments.

There was no room left for her own fear. She retraced her steps to the operating theater.

She'd broken her promise, but she'd finally made her decision. She was following her heart back to Sebastian.

Chapter Thirteen

Leanne sprinted back the way she'd come, holding the gun as if it were a precious talisman. She wouldn't let anyone stop her, no matter what she had to do. The rage that had settled over her when Carla informed her they planned to freeze Sebastian was so all-consuming that she wasn't aware of anything but it driving her on.

The hallways were deserted. Down the stairs she clattered, not caring who heard her. At the scrub room she hesitated, checking it to make sure Carla wasn't lying, to see if by some miracle, he was still hiding there. The room was a shambles. She could tell there'd been a fight, and the locker they'd pushed Betty into was empty.

Suddenly angry voices erupted from the operating room.

"...jeopardize my research!" That was Anthony Montague.

"Leanne's happiness depends on it," William shouted back.

William was here, he would help her! Without hesitation, she burst through the door. Both men whirled toward her in shocked surprise.

Her eyes flew around the room, searching for Sebastian. To one side sat a huge cast-iron tub. It was about a foot off the floor and held Sebastian, immobile, stripped of clothes, half covered with ice, his skin already tinged blue.

''Oh! Sebastian!'' Stumbling across the floor, disregarding the angry voices of the other two men, she dropped the gun beside the tub and began to throw the ice out onto the floor. His lids were closed over his wonderful eyes. His lean sensual lips were purple. She pressed a kiss there, warming them, feeling frantically for a pulse in his neck. It was there, but it was very slow. The ice was doing its job, retarding the metabolic rate.

''I'll get you out of here. I promise you,'' she sobbed, tears streaming uncontrollably down her cheeks.

She grabbed his arms, levering him sideways in the tub so she could heave him over the side to the floor.

He landed hard, facedown. She lay down beside him, turning him to cradle him against her body, her arms wrapped around his shoulders, her legs around his torso, warming him.

Somewhere in her peripheral hearing William and Anthony's voices registered again. They were still arguing.

''Now we have to get rid of both of them,'' Anthony yelled.

''No!''

It was William's roar of anger that momentarily made her glance up. They were struggling, both their faces set in grim determination.

Where was the gun? She glanced down, but it was gone. Somehow, in her effort to get Sebastian out of the tub, she must have kicked the gun beneath it, out of reach.

There was no time to worry about anything else but Sebastian, cradling him against the life-giving warmth of her body. Surely there must be something here to help her, something she could wrap him in. On the wall behind the tub stood some shelving. It was filled with operating sheets, drapes and what looked like some quilted bags. She ran to grab everything she could.

Carefully, she picked up his head and he moaned. She tucked the material under and around him as best she could. Then she rubbed herself against him, using her hands and feet to reach every part. The skin of his cheek was so cold that she could see where her hot tears marked it. She calculated that he couldn't have been in the tub more than twenty minutes. This wasn't severe hypothermia, but he'd also had an obvious blow to the head if the lump at his occipital lobe was any indication. It was important to revive him as soon as possible.

"Sebastian, can you hear me! Sebastian, wake up! I'm here. Everything is all right!" she called to him, placing more tear-washed kisses on the shell of his ear. She blew warm breath into his ear and watched the sensitive skin start to turn pink. "Yes, you're warming up now, aren't you!" A sob broke her laugh of joy. "I know what you need, another hot shower."

A crash brought her head up. She clutched Sebastian even tighter and watched as Anthony Montague fell into a corner. He slumped to the floor, dazed. William stood over him, his chest heaving in exertion.

"Thank God! William, are you all right?"

At her shout he turned slowly. He brushed his mane of white hair from his eyes, composing himself. "Yes, I'm all right. How's Sebastian?"

Amazed at how calm and controlled his voice sounded, Leanne could only nod. "He'll be all right, thanks to you. I'm so grateful you were here to overpower Anthony."

"I'll always be here to help you, Leanne. You know that. Now, let me give Sebastian something to help him."

He reached into a medicine cabinet and turned his back to her for a moment, so she couldn't see what he was doing. Over his shoulder a steady stream of liquid shot into the air. He was purging a needle. Something about his action struck a cord of fear in her.

"What is that, William?"

"Just a stimulant. Something to help him, Leanne." William turned slowly, bearing down on them.

Sebastian shifted slightly in her arms and moaned again. Leanne pressed another kiss to his lips, which were returning to a healthy red. "He's coming around. He doesn't need anything, William."

When she glanced up, he stood over them with a cardiac needle grasped in his hand. "William, he doesn't need a heart stimulant, he's coming to. Just get me some blankets.''

During this day, she had experienced so many emotions—everything from joy to fear to horror—now she didn't think she had the capacity to feel any more. But the look in William's eyes as he gazed down at her struck terror into her very soul.

"Did you know, Leanne, that the most distressing intellectual discovery we make during our lifetimes is that we are physically mortal, presently subjected to a pitifully short span of years? I remember the exact moment I realized I would some day no longer exist, that my consciousness would be no more.'' He smiled the magnificent smile that had mesmerized not only her, but everyone in Peaceful.

"I was born with the gift of imagination. I could see life that was devoid of pain, frustration and turmoil. In such a utopia, death would have no part. So I began my search for immortality."

As he spoke, she inched away, dragging Sebastian out of his reach. Sebastian's eyelashes fluttered, and his lips moved ever so slightly, but he still hadn't fully awakened.

"William, I—I know how you feel about death. You taught us to hold it at bay for as long as possible. Death is the enemy, William.'' Staring up into his face, she finally understood the secrets within. Sebastian had been right. She crouched protectively over him. "William, death is the enemy. You can't help it."

He shook his head, still smiling gently. "No, Leanne, time is the enemy. Do you know when I first recognized that?''

He paused as if expecting her to reply, so she shook her head. Her heart was pounding so loudly that she trembled.

"When I met you, Leanne. I'd devoted myself to medicine, to my research, and suddenly you walked into my classroom and I realized what I'd missed. With you by my side, the days I searched for perfection would have been their own utopia. But time was against us. The years and years I'd been on this earth before you separated us. Then time played more tricks." He knelt, so they were nearly at eye level. "Even though you're always telling me what fine physical shape I'm in, I know my years are diminishing. When I heard about Anthony's research, I felt as if there was hope at last. Hope to achieve my dream. Hope that we could truly be together the way we should have been."

"William, suspended animation isn't possible." Through her overwhelming fear and pain she spoke calmly, as if they were merely involved in another of their medical discussions. She'd been a naive fool. Now, with her eyes opened, she saw down through the years. She had been blinded by her adoration and respect. William was obsessed with her.

"But Anthony is on the very verge of breaking that ice barrier, Leanne!" Enthusiasm enriched his voice, animating his face. "His new combination of chemicals greatly lessens the destruction of tissue. We could be preserved, both of us, resting together, until cures are found for aging. Perhaps someone may find a way to reverse the aging process! Do you know what that could mean for us, Leanne? At last we could be together in a perfect world.''

She shook her head as her eyes filled with tears. Her gaze locked with his intense stare. "William, it isn't possible. We don't have the technology. Those people in the cryotorium are dead. Nothing we do will ever bring them back."

"Anything is possible! Look at transplants. They were hardly successful until the discovery of cyclosporine, and that's only been within the last few years. It *is* possible, Leanne. It *will* happen." His voice became harsh. "But, I don't have time to wait for the slow methodical progress of conventional science. Anthony is a pioneer who knows risks must be taken. The only way to discover if the chemicals make reanimation possible is to test them on humans."

She gasped to cover the fact that Sebastian was beginning to stir. She couldn't let William see that very soon Sebastian would be fully conscious.

He reacted to her apparent horror by giving her another of his patent smiles. "Surely, Leanne, you know I wouldn't risk your life. I assure you, by the time you're ready for interment Anthony's experiments will be complete. But we can't let anything interfere with his experiment, so I'm afraid Sebastian will have to be eliminated. Your future happiness depends on it. Let go of him, my dear. I promise this will be painless for him. It's morphine."

"No! You can't!" Covering Sebastian's body she glared up at him. "I won't let you hurt him!"

Slowly William rose from the floor until he towered over her. "Leanne, I must. I know you will understand and share my enthusiasm once you have time to think through all the implications of this research."

With her back to the tub, she loosened one hand from the grip she had on Sebastian's shoulder. She groped under the tub. With her fingertips, she could barely touch the handle of the gun.

"Leanne, I said let go of Sebastian. You'll soon forget all about him once we start contemplating all our endless tomorrows together."

Stretching so she felt the strain through every muscle of her body, Leanne inched the gun toward her, until she nearly had it grasped between her fingers.

"Leanne, I'm afraid you're going to be angry with me, but I must remove Sebastian from your arms."

He leaned over as if to touch Sebastian. At the same moment, she pulled out the gun and pointed it at him.

"Don't make another move, William. I warn you. I won't let you hurt him!" She was crying so hard she was shaking. Her breathing was short and shallow, the pain inside too great for anything more. How could this be happening? "Please just stop this and go away. Please, William."

His smile was so gentle that her insides ripped with sadness for all that had been, for all he had ever been.

"I've never failed you, have I, Leanne? You must trust me to do the right thing for you. Put the gun down. You know you could never hurt me. We love one another and always will."

He stepped toward her and with shaking hands she aimed the gun. Sebastian stirred against her, shaking his head, shifting his body involuntarily.

William leaned over, the needle poised menacingly.
"No!" Leanne screamed.

Startled, Sebastian's legs convulsed powerfully, striking William's ankles. Swaying wildly, trying to regain his balance, William staggered. With a gasp, he tumbled over Leanne and Sebastian. She threw herself across Sebastian's chest as William fell. When she heard the grunt of pain, she wasn't sure if it came from her own lips, Sebastian's or William's.

William sprawled motionless beside her. Laying Sebastian's head gently on the sheets, she pressed kisses on his eyes. They were fluttering open.

"You're going to be fine. Wait here." Crawling, she reached William and felt for the pulse at his throat. Paralyzed with pain, she sat with one hand futilely on his neck, the other still clutching the gun. She couldn't even move when she heard Anthony come to.

He stumbled toward them and turned William over.

"He fell on the needle."

He, too, felt for a pulse, his eyes staring into her face. "William is dead."

She was so numb she no longer even feared Montague. But when the door whooshed open, she scooted back across the floor toward Sebastian who was struggling up to his elbows, still groggy. The room filled with Sheriff Sullivan, Lewis, Mary and Carla. For one heartbeat, her hand tightened on the gun, then she saw that Carla wore handcuffs.

"What in the hell is going on here!"

"William is dead." Her words were met by Mary's scream. Mary tore across the floor and knelt beside him, sobbing.

"How in the hell did this happen? According to Lewis here, it's you and Sebastian who are in mortal danger." The sheriff's small eyes shifted in his puffy face and finally came to rest on her.

"It—it was an accident." She couldn't say the words, she couldn't quite believe them yet. William, a man who had dedicated his life to saving lives, would have taken one because he loved her.

"Is there time, Dr. Montague? Is there time to save him?" Mary's pleas were heartbreaking. Even though she thought she had no more to shed, tears came again to Leanne's eyes.

"Save him! You mean he's not dead? Then why in the hell aren't all you doctors doing something?" the sheriff bellowed.

"She means, is there time to put him in suspended animation," Leanne explained.

The sheriff shook his head, and looked at Lewis. "Is that what you've been raving about? Frozen corpses, like in a sci-fi movie?"

"They're doing it here, Sheriff Sullivan. Plus a lot more."

"A lot more? What are you talking about, Leanne?" Mary's tear-ravaged face stared up at her. "It's not illegal to be cryonically interred. William told us so. It was his wish, Leanne. You can't deny him his death wish. Not after everything he has meant to you."

"I must start the procedure immediately." Dr. Montague rose to his feet as if nothing else mattered. "Any more delays and the damage caused by lack of blood flow would be irreversible. I'll need Carla to assist me.''

"Seems to me Carla is under arrest. And it seems to me that you probably are, too, Dr. Montague.'' The sheriff shrugged his beefy shoulders and looked toward Leanne. Every eye in the room rested on her face.

Hearing a movement behind her, she looked around as Sebastian pushed to his feet, a sheet fixed securely around his waist. She backed up, until he was leaning against her. His arms were weak, but he was holding her.

"Leanne, please,'' Mary begged, her pale face ravaged by grief.

Her own tears nearly blinding her, Leanne shook her head. "Mary, it doesn't work. We don't have the technology. Nothing will bring William back.''

A shadow of Mary's old spirit brought her chin up, her eyes suddenly determined. "I know. I've always known. But for what he once was, grant him his last request, even if it is meaningless.''

Where the decision came from Leanne didn't know, she just knew she could do nothing else. "Let them do it, Sheriff Sullivan.''

"Quick, Lewis, help me lift him to the table. Sheriff, I must have Carla's assistance!'' Montague barked out orders, assuming control.

Lewis rushed to help him while Sheriff Sullivan unlocked Carla's handcuffs. "Just remember, nobody's leaving this room.''

Even in defeat, Carla managed a sarcastic sneer before she rushed around the room wheeling equipment to the table. They stripped William's clothes, just as they had Sebastian's, and threw a cooling pad under the body.

Sebastian's arms tightened and she looked up through a blur of tears. "All of this is my fault." The whisper rasped through her aching throat.

"Leanne, I'm not clear on everything going on here, but I'd guessed at William's feelings. I do know one thing for sure. You aren't to blame." His fingers gripped her chin, forcing her face up to his. "His obsession isn't your fault. You gave William so much. You aren't to blame because he wanted more."

"I want to believe that. More than anything!"

He slid his fingers down her throat to gently massage the back of her neck. She rested her head on his shoulder, trying to work through all that she'd learned, all that she felt.

"Leanne, you don't have to watch this." Sebastian's voice was full of concern. His whole bearing surrounded her with that spark of protective energy.

"No, I have to be here. Then maybe I can understand and put it behind me."

"First the ventilator. We have to keep as much oxygen in the tissue as we can," Dr. Montague explained as he worked. He spoke as if he were the Creator, laying his accomplishment before them.

With Sebastian's arms supporting her, Leanne stepped closer, until she could see William.

"Now the heart-lung machine pumps a glycerol solution through the veins to block the changes that occur when blood flow stops."

When the transfusion was complete the team rolled the gurney over to the ice tub that had held Sebastian.

"Turn on the nitrogen," said Montague.

Carla flipped a switch and the bottom of the tub instantly frosted.

"All right. Time to move him." Carefully, Carla, Lewis and Montague lifted William's body. It was still attached to the ventilator and the heart-lung machine. They placed him in the tub and packed more ice on top of him.

Montague turned to a small refrigerator and pulled an IV bag out. "This is it," he announced to no one in particular. "This is the elixir of life." He hooked it up to the lines already running into William's body.

Leanne shivered. Sebastian's arms closed around her even tighter. There wasn't a sound in the room until Carla rolled over a stand of equipment. Dr. Montague picked out a scalpel and drew a line down William's chest. Mary gasped.

"I think I'll wait outside the door," Sheriff Sullivan said, leading Mary away.

Montague and Carla worked together efficiently and silently, as if they had done this many times before. The rib cutter finally opened the chest cavity wide enough to expose William's heart. Montague attached an empty tube to the aorta while Carla did the same to the atrium. They closed up the chest cavity and hooked the tubes to an elaborate machine Leanne didn't recognize. While they worked, Lewis kept refilling the ice bath until the body took on an almost alabaster glaze.

"Perfusate," Montague demanded and Carla flipped another switch. Carefully monitoring the controls, he watched the chemical levels as the body began to freeze.

Leanne forced herself to continue watching, but when they placed William's body in a plastic bag, she closed her eyes and shuddered.

"It'll take about twenty minutes to get the body temp down to minus one hundred degrees Fahrenheit. I need to go to the cryotorium to prepare a vault," Montague said.

Leanne nodded wordlessly, and stepped out of Sebastian's arms. She opened the door. "Sheriff, we need you. Take Dr. Montague to the cryotorium. But first handcuff Carla to something."

Mary came to the door, her eyes red from weeping and handed Sebastian his clothes so he could dress. He slid into his slacks and shirt. Leanne needed him beside her, needed his strength and somehow he realized that.

When Montague returned, the sheriff seemed slightly pale and definitely subdued behind him. "It's time to place him in the container now. We'll need Lewis."

In the end, they were all present. Carla and Montague wrapped a cryonic sleeping bag around the plastic bag and attached it to a halter. The tubes were all sealed and disconnected from the machines.

They rolled the gurney into the cryotorium. Lewis operated a ceiling hoist that hooked a halter. The body was lifted straight up and then slowly lowered head-first, into the cylinder. When the cylinder was closed

and sealed, liquid nitrogen flowed into an outer vac-
uum tube that would keep the body at the required
temperature.

Sheriff Sullivan breathed a long, hard sigh of relief. "I think it's time for the doctors and me to take a
little ride to the jail. Lewis, put these other cuffs on Dr.
Montague."

Montague looked at the sheriff with complete dis-
dain. "That won't be necessary." He flicked a cool
look around the room. "You haven't won, you know.
Some day I'm going to bring them all back. You'll
see."

Carla took Dr. Montague's arm with a smile and
gave Leanne one last sarcastic look before being led
out by the sheriff.

"Dr. Hunt?" Lewis stopped in front of them,
nervously twisting his mustache. "Cryonic interment
ain't illegal. What's goin' to happen to Billy and all the
others?"

"There are legitimate organizations in Michigan and
California that operate cryotoriums. We'll notify one
and they will take over the care of these bodies," Sebastian answered slowly.

"Then I can still be frozen with Billy?"

Sebastian nodded and Lewis looked so relieved that
Leanne smiled at him gently. Hope was such a powerful emotion; even false hope carried some dignity.

When they were finally alone, Leanne stepped out
of Sebastian's arms and walked slowly to the glass
porthole. She stared down at the magnificent mane of
pure white hair, at the strong, proud bones of William's face, and at the mouth that had so often smiled

with kindness at her. At her first sight of him, she'd thought he looked like a god. It was what he had sought to be, for who else could offer immortality? Would the world be a better place if men could really offer such a promise? Or would it be a curse?

She leaned toward the porthole for the last time. "Rest in peace, William."

Then she walked straight back into Sebastian's waiting arms. He held her close while she wept for Arthur, William, Marcus, Billy, and all the other people who, out of desperation, had reached for an impossible dream. Life was so short, so unpredictable. Her own, she thought now, must be lived to the fullest while she held it in her hands.

Flinging back her head she peered into the face of the man she loved. "All these people aren't going to have any tomorrows, are they?"

With gentle fingers, he brushed her hair from her forehead, his touch wiping away tears from her cheek. He caressed her trembling mouth. "I don't think so, Leanne. I'll get a court order to have all these records transferred to NASA, but from what I've seen, Montague's research is no further along than our own."

She nodded, searching his face. "I let them go through the motions for Mary . . . for all William once was . . . even knowing it was useless. Somehow—" her voice broke and she fought to steady it "—somehow it seemed like the right thing to do. He wanted us to be together for eternity. But he'll be alone."

Sebastian cupped her cheeks carefully, his fingers splaying across her tear-stained skin. She closed her eyes, a sob catching in her throat as his lips brushed her trembling mouth.

"Open your eyes, Leanne."

She obeyed his soft command.

"I promise, my darling, we will have all the tomorrows that are our due."

He led her out of the cryotorium, up through the control room, where the monitor blinked, keeping an everlasting vigil. With each step, she felt the horror fade. In the hallway, he pressed a kiss to her mouth. He looked at her with eyes that made the pain fade and happiness rush into its place.

"Let's go home," he whispered, taking her chin in strong fingers.

"I live here. You live on the Cape. Where's home?"

His eyes told her everything she'd ever need to know.

"Wherever we're together."

COMING NEXT MONTH

#193 TRIAL BY FIRE by Rebecca York
43 Light Street
Though the Graveyard Murders happened in modern
Baltimore, they were linked to an old evil—black magic.
Herbalist Sabrina Barkley knew little about witchcraft, but
she and assistant D.A. Dan Cassidy feared their meeting in
the investigation was fated. The murders opened a door to
the past—a door they'd have to go through the fires of hell
to close. If they *ever* could . . .

#194 NOWHERE TO HIDE by Jasmine Cresswell
The only survivor of a fiery plane crash, Alyssa Humphrey
was lucky to be alive. But she'd lost her memory. The
Denver mansion no longer seemed like home; her fiancé
seemed a stranger. In a world where everything was
unfamiliar, financial advisor Adam Stryker was the only
man she could trust. Or was he?

#195 WHISTLEBLOWER by Tess Gerritsen
On a foggy highway, Cathy Weaver's headlights lit the
shadowy form of a man too late to avoid hitting him.
Victor Holland had the eyes of a hunted man—and a story
that sounded like the paranoid ravings of a madman. But
his kisses tasted of desperation and desire. Was he a man in
danger . . . or a dangerous man?

#196 CHILD'S PLAY by Bethany Campbell
Thornton Fuller was a young man with a child's mind who
knew a secret about death. When he told the children of
Rachel Dale and Jay Malone, Thornton knew he was in
trouble. Summer residents Rachel and Jay thought evil
couldn't touch idyllic Black Bear Lake. But they were
wrong. Even small towns had their demons. . . .

JAYNE ANN KRENTZ

A two-part epic tale from one of today's most popular romance novelists!

Dreams
Parts One & Two

The warrior died at her feet, his blood running out of the cave entrance and mingling with the waterfall. With his last breath he cursed the woman— told her that her spirit would remain chained in the cave forever until a child was created and born there....

So goes the ancient legend of the Chained Lady and the curse that bound her throughout the ages—until destiny brought Diana Prentice and Colby Savager together under the influence of forces beyond their understanding. Suddenly they were both haunted by dreams that linked past and present, while their waking hours were filled with danger. Only when Colby, Diana's modern-day warrior, learned to love, could those dark forces be vanquished. Only then could Diana set the Chained Lady free....
